Mehded Maryam Sinclair

When Wings Expand

THE ISLAMIC FOUNDATION

WHEN WINGS EXPAND
Published by THE ISLAMIC FOUNDATION
Markfield Conference Centre, Ratby Lane, Markfield
Leicestershire, LE67 9SY, United Kingdom
E-mail: publications@islamic-foundation.com
Website: www.islamic-foundation.com

Distributed by
KUBE PUBLISHING LTD
T +44 (01530) 249230, info@kubepublishing.com
Website: www.kubepublishing.com

Book design | typesetting | illustrations © Fatima Jamadar

Editors Fatima D'Oyen | Yosef Smyth

The publishers would like to thank Nuh Keller for kind permission to reproduce Qur'anic
translations on pages 9–10 and 170–171.

A Cataloguing-in-Publication Data record for this book is available from the British Library

ISBN 978-0-86037-499-2
eISBN 978-0-86037-501-2

Printed by Imak Ofset, Turkey

To Fatima D'Oyen, who saw the possibilities

and set me on the path.

Special thanks to Besa Krasniqi and Nuh Keller, without whose guidance and assistance I could never have written this book. To the Turks I know and love, especially Sevinc, for teaching me hidden treasures. To Patricia Gauch and Kim Griswold for their expert comments and edits. To Kent Brown, for the opportunities he threw my way. To Reema Latif for being willing to go through every page looking for what could be better. To the Muslim Writers Awards, UK, for choosing the manuscript as a winner, and to Saddia Malek, who helped me collect the prize all the way from Jordan. To Ibrahim, for his rock-solid support. To Jed, for his continued interest and suggestions. To Hedaya Hartford, Amina Ackroyd, Zarlasht, Rohi Padela and all the others who were willing to read, discuss and help in so many ways. To Marshia Choudhury for passing the book on to its first young readers, and to those first readers and their teachers, you know who you are.

Mehded Maryam Sinclair

For more information about the author and her work visit www.maryamsinclair.com

The body exists that
we might grow wings.

Abdal Hakim Murad

...'O Lord, take us not to task if we forget or make a mistake;

O Lord, nor place upon us an unsuperable load as You did on those just before us;

Nor then requite us with what we have no strength to withstand;

But pardon us, forgive us, and show us bounteous mercy,

You are our Master: so give us triumph over the people of the unbelievers.'

- Al Baqarah 2:286 -

Sunday, May 4 | 08

I am Nur, daughter of Firdaus and Yusuf, granddaughter of Halima. I am twelve. I live where I was born, in Toronto, Canada, with my Turkish-Muslim mother. My father Yusuf grew up as an American Quaker, and became Muslim when he was sixteen. My little brother is Mehmed, and he is eight. My mother's mother, Halima, lives in Istanbul and was married to Abdallah, a Moroccan naturalist who died in a car accident in Turkey before I was born. There are more people in my family, of course; I'll write about them later.

A few weeks ago Mama gave me this journal. She bought it for me last year when she went to Quebec City with Baba, just after she found out she had cancer. She said she knew how hard her sickness has been for me. She scared me a little bit when she said that. She said my writing and drawing could be a medicine for me, but I didn't know I needed any medicine so I left it sitting in my drawer until now.

I used to write a lot, but that was before Mama got sick, before the cells in her body decided they would go crazy and do whatever they wanted.

I've never had a journal as beautiful as this one is. I wanted to find the right word for the color of its leather cover, and not just write "blue" … it is a spectacular blue, not at all ordinary so I found "azure" in the thesaurus. Azure blue it is, and it reminds me of the blue stone necklace my friend Hana's dad brought her from Afghanistan. I love staring at the color, trying to climb inside it, where I feel safe and protected. The pages have a tiny little bit of texture. I wonder if this is hand-made paper? Anyway, I like how the book lies flat when it is open so I don't have to fight with it and it is easy to write in it.

This journal really matters to me, so I shall name it. Naming things always makes them more important. From now on its name shall be Buraq.

Ya Buraq, you are sooo cool, can I use your name for my journal? You are the animal the Angel Jibril brought from the heavens and which flew the Prophet Muhammad all the way from Makkah to Jerusalem in one night.

Sunday, May 11 | 08

Dear Buraq, today we were supposed to be going sailing on Yasemin's family's sailboat, Baba, Mehmed, me, and even Mama. The plan was to go out on Lake Ontario. A few days ago Mama was feeling better and she was looking forward to having the wind in her face. But she woke up in the middle of Friday night with a searing headache and by Saturday morning she wasn't able even to lift up her head. Baba was constantly repeating "*la hawla wa la quwatta illa b'illahul azeem*"—there is no power or might save Allah's—and that made me even more scared. The doctor came over right after *fajr*, the early-morning prayer, and said she was having a delayed reaction to her last chemotherapy treatment. Well, why wouldn't she react, getting all pumped up with poison? It is so scary to think about what they have to do to get rid of cancer. Anyway, the doctor came and gave her two injections and the headache went away, *alhamdulillah*. But she still feels weak and dizzy.

Still, she was so sweet to us. Mama was in bed, and Baba was holding her shoulders and stroking her long wavy black hair. She told us she felt sad about being the reason we were missing the trip. Good old Mehmed! He said, "That's OK! Nur gets seasick all the time, and anyway look how gray the day is! It's better we stay home and Mrs. Prouty can make us cookies!" Was this Mehmed talking? If it wasn't for his shiny black hair I would have been sure it was some other child, able to talk like that. Honestly, I never knew he had it in him!

Monday, May 12 | 08

It's a good thing I started doing my homework early on Sunday, because it took me all day! I was supposed to write about "what it would be like to ...." I came up with these ideas:

Live on a fishing boat
Live on an Iroquois reservation
Get a gift of $1000
Paddle a canoe to the Toronto Islands

I wanted to add:
Have breast cancer
Lose your mother
Be like everyone else

But I didn't have the courage to write about those. Especially not the last one, because I am so afraid of being ungrateful. I know we are not like everyone else because we are Turks and we are Muslims. And I know in my heart of hearts that I wouldn't change either of those things for anything. So I say, too bad, Nur, you don't get to be "like everyone else," and guess what? It just doesn't matter! And don't forget, you have plenty of friends who aren't "like everyone else" either! What about Yasemin and her five Turkish brothers? What about Janine from Palestine, and Hana from Afghanistan, what about all the people who go to the Andalusia Mosque, let alone all the other masjids in Toronto?

So what I did write about was getting a gift of $1000. It was really fun! Here's a tiny piece of my homework:

$1000! Yikes! That is so much money! What will I do with it? I didn't realize before what a responsibility money is—just deciding what to do with it is hard work. My first thoughts were all about new clothes and bracelets and necklaces. Then I looked around my room and saw the great maple bed Uncle Furqan built for me, the wicker chair Mama brought me from Quebec, my stained-glass lamp, my luscious cream-colored settee with its dusty pink throw—what more do I need? This much money seems too special to spend like that. Then I thought about taking my family on a vacation, and remembered with a start that Mama is too sick to go anywhere right now. And then it hit me—her medicine! I want to use the money to help buy her medicines! But first I'm going to spend whatever it takes to get her a beautiful new quilt, and some new plants for the window-sill near her bed. I want the quilt to be something that soothes

her and makes her happy just to see it. Since she has to spend so much time in bed these days, let it be with beautiful things around her. She loves colors and fabric and geometry. I pray she likes it.

I got so excited writing this. I quite forgot that it was all a fantasy! Then I remembered that Grandma gave me some money recently. It was $350, not $1000, but I can use it to buy a quilt for Mama! Last year when we went to the county fair there was a booth with home-made quilts. I took one of their flyers, because I had never ever seen anything so beautiful—the colors, the shapes. It made me want to be a quilt maker when I grow up.

I can't wait! I'll get someone to take me to see them and choose the best one I can find for Mama.

Wednesday, May 14 | 08

Every Wednesday afternoon I have a class with Yasemin at the Andalusia Mosque. We are doing an intense study of the Qur'an with Auntie Khadija. She has been teaching us *tajweed*, the proper pronunciation of Arabic, for the last three years. Now that we have nearly mastered the *tajweed* we are reciting the whole Qur'an, memorizing it as we go, and learning the meaning of each page. I've always been really happy doing *tajweed*, but this is a lot harder. First of all, the memorizing is hard, and then sometimes the meanings are even harder. But every once in a while I come across something that just leaves me with a delight I can barely understand. Like,

> *Allah is the Light of the heavens and the earth—*
> *The likeness of His light in hearts guided by those verses is*
> *as a niche in which is a tremendous lighted lamp, the*
> *lamp mounted in a crystal sheath of brightest glass, the*
> *sheath of glass as if an iridescent star—it fueled from*

a tree utterly abundant with blessings, an olive tree

in the day's sun neither solely from the east nor from

the west, whose oil is well-nigh luminous

though yet untouched by fire

- Qur'an: Al-Nur, 34-38 -

Honestly, Buraq, when I found these verses, my world just stopped. The picture they give is so clear! It felt like everything just opened out and out and out, and I was standing all alone on the very edge of the universe. And all of a sudden I remembered the lines from William Blake that we had to memorize and write about in English class. And I knew that it wasn't just nice lines of poetry ... it is what is REAL, only most of the time I can't remember it.

To see a world in a grain of sand

And a heaven in a wild flower,

Hold infinity in the palm of your hand

And eternity in an hour.

- William Blake, Auguries of Innocence -

When I was memorizing the verses from the Qur'an I kept

feeling like something was coming to me, something REAL, something that would nourish me and heal me, and never leave me.

So *this* is what makes Mama and Baba and Grandma so careful to never leave the Qur'an. I pray that I will never leave it, that it will never leave me.

Friday, May 16 | 08

My Auntie Ayshe, Mama's sister, has come from Turkey to stay with us. Sometimes it seems like she is crying. But when she sees me, she will always smile and hug me. It helps me a lot to have those hugs, because something is really strange around here now, and I know it. Nobody's been telling me much, but I can see how worried and sad everybody is. I want somebody to sit down and tell me what is going on, but they are all so busy, and guess what, Buraq? I realize that actually I don't want to be told ... it is too scary.

Monday, May 19 | 08

Buraq, today there were a bunch of announcements hanging on the bulletin board at school about summer camps! Oh, can you imagine being able to spend a week in the forest, paddling canoes and riding horses? I brought one of the flyers home. I knew there's no way my Baba would send me someplace away from him where I would be around men he doesn't know. I read in my friends' magazines how everybody thinks Muslim girls are oppressed, but I can't really figure out what all the fuss is about—I just feel cherished and protected. But I wanted to ask him anyway, to see if by some miracle I could go. Baba didn't say no right away, he said he would talk to Mama and pray so that he could make the best decision, considering everything that is happening with us right now.

Tuesday, May 20 | 08

Today I had my science exam. We got an extra study break before lunch to prepare so Yasemin, Janine, and I crammed a bit beforehand. Janine had already studied a lot with her brother so she was kinda like our coach. I think I did OK on the exam but I know I didn't ace it because I couldn't define "terminal velocity." *Maalesh*, whatever, right, Buraq? I'm so glad I don't have parents who rank on me all the time to get straight A's!

I see how they both love working hard and how they do it remembering Allah, so I am trying to be like them … but working just to get good grades is something else.

Saturday, May 24 | 08

This morning I went to visit Yasemin. I usually don't go to her house because her brothers are around, but they have all gone on a trip with their uncle, so Mama said I could go. I felt guilty leaving her feeling sick, but she insisted, and we had so much fun! They have a tree house in the back yard and we had the place to ourselves. I was a little freaked by the tree-house ladder but I got used to it and then it got easy. It's funny how our brains can make something so simple seem so big and scary. Afterwards we made cheese sandwiches and hibiscus tea. To make the tea we put the hibiscus flowers into a glass jar with water sweetened with honey, and left it on the tree-house porch in the sun.

Of all my friends, Yasemin is the closest. Some people say we look like sisters—we are both on the tall side, and have very dark brown eyes and very thick eyelashes and eyebrows. Maybe we're so similar because her family is so like mine, in a way. Our mothers are best friends. They lived near each other in Turkey, and they both came here because they couldn't bring themselves to uncover their hair to go to university in Turkey. My dad isn't Turkish like

Yasemin's dad though, he's American, so that's different. And I certainly don't have five brothers.

Yasemin's house is one place I can go and find lots of the same kinds of food as we have at home, that's for sure. And her mother Aliya teaches in the university here like my mother does. They used to study together when they were still in Turkey, and now Yasemin and I do that too.

Sunday, May 25 | 08

I didn't have time to write about the story Yasemin told me yesterday about one of the Companions of Muhammad, may Allah bless him and give him peace. Yasemin's father is constantly studying about them and the stories he tells her are so interesting and so different from the ones I have heard. The only thing is that now that I am about to write it down I suddenly can't remember the man's name. Wait, Buraq, let me call her and ask her. I hate it when this happens.

OK, Yasemin has told me. His name is Ziyad ibn as-Sakkan. When he was only eighteen years old he promised that he would protect the Muslims in the Battle of Uhud, when they were fighting to defend Madinah against their enemies from the Quraysh, a tribe that wanted to destroy them. He received so many wounds, and Muhammad held Ziyad's head in his lap while he was dying, and washed the mud from his face with his own tears. He prayed that Allah would accept Ziyad's promise and reward him for it and begged Him to make Ziyad one of His companions in Paradise.

Buraq, I feel so many conflicting things when I hear these

stories. First, I feel sad that I was not living in those times and did not have an opportunity to see it. But there is something else, and it scares me. Would I be among the brave ones, who kept their promises and did not run away in the face of death, or would I be one of those who ran off to protect myself?

Monday, May 26 | 08

Buraq, I aced my science exam! Other than the "terminal velocity" question, I got almost everything else right, thanks to my study session with Yasemin and Janine. Alhamdulillah for such great friends! They both scored higher, but my score was still enough to be an "A". Mama said she was so grateful I like studying!

Tuesday, May 27 | 08

Buraq, Mama is in the hospital again. Something happened in the night, and an ambulance came and took her, with Baba, and they have not come home yet. My little brother Mehmed threw a fit when he woke up and found them gone. He refuses to get ready to go to school. I'd like to help him, but I have more exams today and if I miss school I'll get into trouble. I called Baba. He wanted to talk to Mehmed. I don't know what he said to him, but Mehmed calmed down a lot and when he got off the phone he said that Uncle Furqan, Mama's brother, was coming over to take him to school.

Wednesday, May 28 | 08

I miss Mama. It is so quiet when she is gone. I have to buy her quilt. O Allah, let her come home soon, and let her get better soon, and let me buy the quilt soon—I just know she will love it so much.

Thursday, May 29 | 08

Today Baba is going to take us to visit Mama. This morning
he was talking to Mehmed, who was worrying about going
to the hospital because he is too noisy. Baba assured
him that Mama loves his noise and told him it is her best
medicine. You should have seen his smile!

Monday, June 2 | 08

Hana and her mom came to visit Mama in the hospital after school. I was so happy to see them, and I think Mama was too. She doesn't talk much these days, but I saw her eyes brighten a bit when they walked in. They brought her body butter made with coconut oil and real lavender oil. I put some on her face right away, and she kissed my hand!

After they left it suddenly hit me how sick Mama really is. Buraq, what if she doesn't get better? What if she can't get better? Ever since she first got sick we have all just been waiting for her to get better, but what if...

Tuesday, June 3 | 08

Buraq, we finally got to go to the quilt shop. Auntie Ayshe
and our neighbor Mrs. Prouty took me. Buraq, it is soooo
cool! Quilts are like snowflakes! There's just no end to the
possible combinations of color and shapes. My favorites are
the geometric ones because they are just like the classical
geometry Uncle Furqan was showing me last summer.
Once you start deciding how to divide a circle into parts
it goes on and on and on like a kaleidoscope into infinity.
I saw the quilt that I want to buy for Mama. Its design is
based on a five-pointed star and the colors are lavenders,
blues, creams, pinks, and true greens. I just know she will
love it. When I found out the price I almost fainted. It was
way more expensive than I thought it would be, but when
the lady in the shop heard who I was buying it for she gave
me a huge discount! I love it when people are so generous.
Since the one I saw in the shop was already sold, I have to
order one. They said it would be ready in two weeks but I
said Mama needs it right away. She said she would try to
speed things up.

Wednesday, June 4 | 08

The doctors were saying Mama might come home today, but she is still not strong enough and they don't know why. When Mehmed found out he ran outside and started throwing sticks of wood at the woodpile and yelling, "No! She HAS to come home TODAY!!!" Poor kid ... He was doing exactly what I felt like doing. By the time Baba got out there with him he had fallen on the ground sobbing. Baba sat down next to him and held him for the longest time.

Friday, June 6 | 08

Mehmed and I went for a long walk with Baba in the morning and, Buraq, you'll never guess what we found! A chrysalis! It was just hanging there, on a blackberry bush. Mashallah, it is the most amazing green color ... I just can't stop thinking about the color ... it's not really lime green, and it's not really olive green, and it certainly isn't fresh green or true green. It is a pastel, but I can't think of any other pastel green like it except for maybe one of the pistachios Auntie Ayshe brought us from Turkey. But, no, even that is different. The chrysalis looks like it's made of wax. But the most amazing part of it is that it seems to be wearing a gold necklace! Now, Buraq, when I say gold I am not referring to the color gold, which looks like mustard, I mean the shining glistening gold of jewelry. Can you believe it? On a plant! When I told Baba I just couldn't bear the thought of walking away from it, he grinned and said that when he was a boy in Montana he used to bring chrysalises home and put them in a tank or jar so they could watch them open and release butterflies. Butterflies in your house! We broke the branch carefully and carried it home. It is propped up inside a jar in the kitchen.

Saturday, June 7 | 08 *around noon*

Mama is coming home today, finally! And Buraq, you'll never believe what happened! At 9:30 the doorbell rang, and there was the lady from the quilt shop with a big package. She said she talked with the customer who had already bought the quilt I loved, and she was willing to be the one to wait for the new one instead of me! Buraq, can you believe it? Do you know what this means? It means when Mama comes home this afternoon, her new quilt will be waiting for her on her bed!!!

And, *then*, what a day ...

I found two more chrysalises. I woke up this morning for *fajr*, and while I was praying I told Allah how grateful I am for the chrysalis we found yesterday. I went back to sleep and then I woke up again as the sun was rising and wanted to be in the garden. That's when I found them. One was on the underside of a red cabbage leaf. The other was hanging under a daisy! It feels like now that I have seen one I will see them everywhere.

Saturday, June 7 | 08 after sunset

After lunch Baba went to the hospital to bring Mama home.
Mehmed and I stayed home with Mrs. Prouty. She made
us pancakes and then helped us make a special place for
the chrysalises. What a strange word ... kris-a-liss. We put
them in an empty fish tank lined with soft grass. We had
cut the blackberry branch long, so it could lean across the
inside of the tank, and the chrysalis hung down from it, just
in the middle. We tied the red cabbage leaf to the upper
part of the branch, and put the daisy in a little jar of water
in the bottom of the tank. When we looked in, we could
see all three of them, each in their own little protected
place. We covered the top with a piece of wire screen.

Later Yasemin's mother Aliya came with a huge bunch
of pink and white roses for Mama, with feathery ferns all
through them, in a huge crystal vase. She also brought a
plate of yummy buns.

Mama looks like she is getting better! Alhamdulillah. You
should have seen her, Buraq. Baba brought her in sitting up
in a wheelchair. When she saw the quilt she flipped right
into Turkish like she always does when she is shocked or

surprised. I was sitting on the other side of her bed from the door. Her eyes flew open wide when she saw it, then she looked at me and asked, "*Bu ne, yavrum? Neredan geldi bu? Mashallah!*"–what's this, my little baby? All good things come from Allah! Then she wanted to know where it came from.

She leaned over the bed and looked at it closely. I think she ran her fingers over every single piece of fabric. Then a shining tear slid down her cheek, Buraq. I watched it drop onto the quilt and I reached for it, as if it were a star I could somehow keep. But the tiny wetness seeped into my skin and was gone, and then I started to cry.

She asked me why I was crying. She said, "Look at this beautiful quilt you gave me." Well, that made me cry even harder! For the first time, I felt terrified at the thought of losing her.

She wrapped her arms around me and said, "Nur, *habibti*, my love! I know. I don't want to go. But all I can do is keep trusting in Allah. Nur, I will always be with you! My love and advice will always be with you to guide you in the right direction." She patted my heart. "They are forever sealed inside this little place. And do you have any idea how happy you have made me with this quilt?"

Oh, Buraq, I loved her so much in that minute! I took her hand and pressed it to my wet cheek. I couldn't believe

how happy it made me that I had given her something
she liked so much.

Sunday, June 8 | 08

Mrs. Prouty comes over every day. Mashallah, she always has something sweet to give us, and then she starts cleaning the house. She always begins in Mama's room. Auntie Ayshe helps Mama now. Before she went in to hospital, Ayshe helped her go into the bathroom to wash her face and hands and sit under the shower. While she was in there, Mrs. Prouty would change the sheets on Mama's bed and dust the little tables next to the bed. Sometimes she would polish the windows, and every day she would run the vacuum cleaner around and under the bed. She would bring fresh flowers from her garden, and when Auntie Ayshe brought Mama out of the bathroom, Mama would always say, "Mashallah, Mrs. Prouty, what have you done in here? It looks like the angels have come! Your flowers smell so good. They are my best medicine."

But now, even with Auntie Ayshe's help, Mrs. Prouty can't help Mama get up anymore. Now they wash her hands and face in the bed with big white fluffy towels, and when Auntie Ayshe rolls Mama to one side of the bed, Mrs. Prouty untucks the sheet from the other side. They roll her over the fold in the middle, and then Auntie Ayshe pulls the sheet free on her side. Today they brought a fluffy white sheepskin to put under the sheets. Mama told me to come feel it and asked me where I thought it came from. Buraq, that is when I saw how thin she has become. Her bones were showing through her skin.

Monday, June 9 | 08

My little brother Mehmed can't reach the chrysalis tank but he can see through the glass. At first we looked every day, but they always looked the same. After a while we forgot about them and stopped looking. But today he came running into Mama's room. "Nura, come quick! One of the chrysalises looks really strange!"

I went to look. It really was strange. It had gone dark! I felt so sad when I saw that the lovely green color and the little golden necklace were gone, and I started to cry. Baba heard me and came to see.

"Aha!" he said. He took off his glasses and polished them, and then looked closely. "Yep, things are just as they should be, my little pet. Ahhh, come here, sweetie." He sat down and held me close and I buried my head in his shoulder.

First Mama's bones, and then it was my lovely chrysalis. It was so ugly! I should never have brought it inside, I told Baba.

He stroked my head and held me for a long time and kept repeating greetings to Prophet Muhammad and rocking me back and forth. Mehmed came and pushed himself up onto his lap too.

I told him I was afraid of how thin Mama had become, of how I could see her bones. I started to cry again and I could feel Baba's voice catch in his throat, and then I saw there were tears in his eyes.

After a long time, he asked us if we trusted him. "Of course, Baba," we said.

He said he wanted to tell us something very important. Did we remember the butterflies we saw the other day in the garden? Could we imagine that one day they were each once inside a chrysalis like the ones we found?

He pointed out that if Allah had left the chrysalis the way it was, all adorned with a gold necklace, there would be no butterfly! And with no butterflies there would be no new chrysalises.

Well, Mehmed wanted to know why. "Can't he just make more whenever He wants to?"

Baba chuckled. He said, of course, but Allah has made everything in a pattern. He said people are part of that pattern too. Just like chrysalises don't stay the same, people don't stay the same either. He tousled our hair and teased us. He asked Mehmed if he always wanted to be a little boy like he is now, and Mehmed punched him playfully.

He said maybe the chrysalis doesn't look as pretty as it once did, but we should wait a little while, and we will see that Allah will make something wonderful happen to it, and when we see it, he said we wouldn't mind these dark days so much.

Tuesday, June 10 | 08

You know, Buraq, everything Baba said about the chrysalis really is true! This afternoon I looked closely at it and I could see a folded monarch butterfly's wing inside. The other chrysalis just looked the same as it did before. Baba carried the tank into Mama's room in the morning and we all sat, watching. Mrs. Prouty brought us a big tray of cheese, cucumbers, tomatoes, and home-made biscuits for breakfast.

We watched all morning. First, the chrysalis seemed to get a bit fatter. It started to look like something wrapped in a dark and dry onion skin. Then we noticed that skin had torn open. Finally the butterfly fell to the floor of the tank, all folded up. The empty shell was left hanging from the branch. At first I thought the butterfly was dead, but then its wings began to peel open. Still, I was sure something must be wrong with it. It looked like a big fat June bug, not a butterfly!

Mama smiled and told me she loves how I always notice things.

Baba told me to just wait and watch.

Mrs. Prouty brought tea for us and medicine for Mama.

The wings began to quiver. The body began to pulse like blood was running through it. Soon the wings were all the way open. It looked so silly, with two scrawny little wings and a big fat body—this poor butterfly would never be able to fly anywhere!

But then I noticed that things were changing. The body began to shrink, and the wings began to grow. I looked again, could it really be? But it was true—the body was already a little smaller, and the wings were already a bit bigger.

After almost two hours the body was as thin as a twig and the wings were wide and strong. Then they began to flutter. It was getting ready to fly!

Baba wanted to take the tank out. He asked a question that made me laugh. "Why should a butterfly want to fly around inside our house?"

I didn't want him to take the tank out at first, but when I thought about that poor butterfly tearing its wings on our curtain rods, I told him to put it out on Mama's porch so we could all watch it fly away.

It stayed where it was for a long time, fluttering its wings and getting ready. It was a good thing that big fat body shrank! How would the butterfly ever have lugged it around?

Then it happened! The butterfly flew! First it just flew from the floor of the tank to the top edge. It stayed there for a long time, fluttering, fluttering, and then it flew away from the tank and sat on the porch railing. Oh, I didn't want it to go! I wanted it to be mine, and stay with me always! But when it flew away from the porch and into the pear tree, my heart warmed to see it fluttering there on one of the branches, doing exactly what Allah had created it to do.

I looked at Mama's bony wrists. *Her body is shrinking...*

I feel scared.

But I trust Allah.

Thursday, June 12 | 08

I am writing before I even get out of bed because
something really strange is going on. I don't know where
my dreams begin and where they end. I dreamed I saw
Mama and she had wings! Her body was as thin as a wisp
and she had wings that glowed. I woke up in the middle of
the night after the dream and went into her room. Baba was
sleeping. I think I saw the wings on her!

She was awake, and she saw me, and she whispered something to me. I could barely hear her, so I put my face right
beside hers. She smelled so good, like every flower that ever
was. Buraq, I just have to tell you every word she said:

"Nurajik, don't be afraid. I am not afraid. I saw Prophet
Muhammad and Prophet Jesus, and they said, 'We will
watch out for your girl.' Nur …"

Then she couldn't speak any more. She tried to draw me
closer but she wasn't strong enough, so I snuggled closer
to her. Then she closed her eyes and rested.

I fell asleep there, on my knees with my face beside hers,
but I woke up here, in my own bed, Buraq. I'm sure I went

into her bed, and I remember being there with my face
beside hers, but I don't know how I returned to my bed.
I could never have left her.

Friday, June 13 | 08

We were beginning to wonder if the second chrysalis I found a couple of weeks ago would ever change. I don't know how old it was when I found it, but they usually change in about ten days. We waited thirteen and a half days. I was so worried about it! My science teacher Mr. Jameson said it might just have been too early to collect them and then I really got frantic.

I kept thinking about what Baba said to me when the first chrysalises turned black. I guess I really would be sad if the chrysalis just stayed there and never changed, even though I love how it looks. Later I told Baba what I was thinking. He kissed my hair and said how proud he was of me. Then he looked at the floor. He told me that Mama is getting sicker, and that the doctors can't find a way to cure her. I'll never know where my words came from, but I asked him if she was going to die. He said only Allah knows, but it seems it may be soon ... and then there were lots of tears and his face was all wet and I kissed him and they were salty and my throat ached like it had a big hot rock stuck in it.

The heat from that rock burned all the way through me. If Allah loved us, He would not let her die.

Baba knew what I was thinking. He always did. He told me I must understand that Allah knows more than we do. We cannot decide what should or should not happen. We have done all we know how to do, and she hasn't gotten better. His voice dropped to a whisper, and he said, "Soon the rest of our family will come to see her, to say goodbye to her."

My throat hurt and my stomach churned. I told him I knew her body was shrinking.

Baba's eyes grew wide. "What?"

I told him I can see her body is shrinking by the way her bones stick out of her wrists. Then I told him about the dream I had last night, about the glimpse I caught of her wings—and do you know, Buraq, *he's* the reason I ended up in my own bed! He found me in Mama's bed and carried me back to it. So that's what happened, Buraq! I *had* been with Mama after all!

Baba said it was an incredible, magnificent dream—those are the words he used. He said it's a good sign whenever a Muslim sees a prophet in a dream, and Mama has seen two talking about me in the same dream.

Two prophets telling my mother they will look out for me... It gives me chills, Buraq.

Friday, June 13 | 08 *evening*

Mama's friends came to read the Qur'an to her today. Mama was so happy to see them, and especially grateful that they came to recite the Qur'an. She always listens to the Qur'an whenever she gets a chance. Yasemin, Hana, and Janine came too, with their moms. They brought gifts for her. Yasemin's mother Aliya brought her a beautiful gold bracelet. Hana's mother had brought her a hand-made lace handkerchief, and Janine's mother brought the most beautiful pure cotton nightgown with pink roses on it. Mrs. Prouty baked chocolate cakes and she let us help her grate the chocolate, scrape the vanilla pods, and whip the cream.

After eating we sat and read the Qur'an together again and then we sang some sacred songs. We were singing a new one Janine's mom taught us when Mehmed ran in.

The other chrysalis had opened, and the butterfly was just about to fly away.

But it was a black, stormy Friday. The rain lashed the windows in Mama's room. How would the butterfly fly in the rain? How?

Then Mama said we should put the tank in the garage with the door up so the butterfly could fly without going out into the rain. That's what we did. We wanted to wait around and see what it would do, but we were busy with our guests. Later we found the tank empty, and we never saw the butterfly again.

Saturday, June 14 | 08

Oh, I wish I could reproduce that chrysalis green. I've tried for hours but I must not have the right paint. Even if I could find the color, I don't know how I'd paint its waxy feel. And even though I have metallic gold paint now, the little golden necklace will just never look the same.

Monday, June 16 | 08

For two years we have all been praying that Mama's treatments would make her better, and they haven't. I hate the treatments, Buraq. I hate the hospital, and the pathetic doctors who can't even cure my mother, even though she does everything they say and more.

But you know something strange, Buraq? I can see those hates, but there's a place in me nothing can touch. I mean, two weeks ago, I felt scared about being mad at Allah. I even looked at Mama, and I thought, why is she still going through so much to say every prayer? Why is she still trying so hard to pray at night? Why is she still reading her Qur'an? What did all that do for her? I was afraid about these thoughts, ashamed of them, but I wasn't bitter inside. I could never have brought myself to write them down, even to you, Buraq, whom I know I can trust more than anyone in the world.

Now, everything has changed for me. First, the chrysalis, the poor, pathetic ugly black chrysalis, the one that used to be so beautiful ... I mean, somebody could just get stuck on the beautiful green chrysalis and never want it to change and lose its color. But then they would never see that its loss brought something even more amazing; the butterfly.

I opened up a grapefruit yesterday and found a seed that had sprouted! It already had two tiny folded leaves and I thought, by the time these leaves are big, the seed will have practically disappeared. But what could be better than a new grapefruit tree, and all those new grapefruits? Ever since I was born Mama and Baba and Grandma have told me that we are only here for a little while, and then we will go on to something else.

I'm finally getting it, Buraq. Mama is shrinking because something else, something I can't see, is expanding! Like the butterfly's wings expand inside the black chrysalis so it can fly.

Wednesday, June 18 | 08

Today Mehmed and I had a big fight. He was being so rude and I had zero, nil, nada patience with him, so I screamed at him. He screamed back and threw a glass of milk at me. I don't even remember why he was being rude. And I don't remember fighting with him like that before. It really surprised me. I felt like, well, if Mama's gonna die then the whole house is broken anyway, so it doesn't matter if I shout back. Buraq, how could I feel that after all those things I wrote the other day? I must be some kind of beast or something.

Anyway, Baba took us to the waterfall at Belfountain Conservation Center after he came home. He wanted us to tell him what happened from the beginning. I told him I was ashamed for letting myself get involved in the fight like that. He was so kind, Buraq. He said this is a really hard time for us all, and it isn't surprising that we are losing control, but that we have to try really hard to keep loving each other, because that is the thing that will help us the most. He said if Mama dies, we will all still be here looking at each other, and we have to be ready to help each other.

Monday, June 23 | 08

Today some nurses came with big bottles and tubes and beeping things. Mama's room seems like a hospital room now. I can't believe how much all those beeping things change the feeling in there. When I go in I just want to rip them out. Mrs. Prouty stays all day now, she only goes home to sleep and then she is back, puttering around quietly in the kitchen fixing breakfast for us. I love her. She really cares about us and right now we need so much help.

Friday, June 27 | 08

Today was the last day of school. I cried and cried. So many of my friends are leaving for the summer, and I feel like my life will be empty without them. Even before Mama got sick I hated the end of school because it meant the end of Janine for the summer and usually of Hana too. I always miss them in the summer anyway, but this year it feels so much worse. But then, do you know what happened, Buraq? After school I went out into the garden and I saw this huge beautiful daisy. I looked closer, and hanging from it was a chrysalis! I brought it inside and put it in the tank in a little glass of water.

Thursday, July 3 | 08

Baba's friends came after *maghrib*, and Uncle Furqan, and Yasemin's dad Uncle Uthman, with a big drum—his *bendir*, from Turkey. They sat in the front room and sang sacred songs from Turkey and Morocco and recited the Qur'an. Most of the songs Uncle Uthman has been singing since he was a little boy. He even started playing the *bendir* when he was only six. They were all crowded into the room sitting on the floor in a big circle together and while they were singing, Mehmed just could not sit still. He was dancing around the outside of the circle with Yasemin's brothers! Actually, even I was dancing around in the kitchen when I was making their salads. Mrs. Prouty made them big trays of rice and chicken. I kept going in to see Mama and she was delighted! They sang in Turkish and Arabic mostly, with a couple of English songs.

Friday, July 4 | 08

I went back to sleep after *fajr* and woke up an hour later
when my Uncle Furqan came into my room with a bunch of
balloons tied with ribbon. He said he had to pick up Uncle
Daoud and Auntie Sulma from the airport and wanted me
to go with him. I didn't want to get up, but I could smell
Mrs. P's sticky buns and I was really hungry!

When I went downstairs the doctor was in Mama's room.
He was talking in a low voice to Baba, and Baba was just
looking out the window. He didn't see me and I didn't hear
anything except, "Maybe not more than a few days."

Uncle Furqan scooped me up and took me out to see his
new blue car. As beautiful as it is, I couldn't even look at it.

What was the doctor saying to Baba? I wanted to ask but I
felt like someone had just poured cement into my stomach,
so I just decided to pretend I hadn't heard anything. I could
hardly eat anything when we were back inside. I love maple
syrup sticky buns, but I just couldn't get my mouth to open.
It was all I could do to just sit at the table and pretend
everything was OK. Mrs. Prouty looked at me and somehow

she seemed to know that something was really bothering me. As soon as we could get away, Mehmed and I got in the fancy blue car, Uncle Furqan opened the roof, and we drove off to the airport. When I felt all that wind around me, and the sun beating down on me, I started to feel a little better. It was a big change to be speeding down the road and that's just what I needed.

Saturday, July 5 | 08

The tubes and beeping things were all gone when we got back from the airport. Mama was propped up on pillows. She was happy to see her brother Daoud. She couldn't get up or anything but her eyes were happy, even though they were full of tears. Daoud's were too, even though he was smiling and teasing her about what a tough big sister she had been for him.

Uncle Daoud and Auntie Sulma brought us so many presents! They brought bicycles for me and Mehmed. My uncles put them together right away last night and we got to ride them around in front of the house for a while in the dark.

Today all day long more and more people came to our house.

At the late afternoon prayer it was so crowded that the men prayed together out on the back lawn instead of going to the mosque.

Tuesday, July 8 | 08

I woke up before everyone else was awake and went into Mama's room. Oh, it was so nice to have all that stuff out of there! Mama wanted me to hug her. She smelled of lavender oil from a sachet she had, and Baba's fragrant oud oil. She was having trouble talking but she told me that I must try and remember that Allah is the One who makes things happen and we don't need to be afraid, because He never allows anything to happen that is not the best for us. It's just that we can't see everything so we might not understand at the time. "Wait. Wait and watch," she told me. "You will see, Allah is cherishing you."

Wednesday, July 9 | 08

Our house has never seen such days, Buraq. Every room is full of people praying and reading the Qur'an and singing sacred songs. Baba told me Mama is in pain, and the Qur'an has secrets to help to relieve her pain. And he said she will be making a great journey, and she will need the kind of help that only the Qur'an can give.

Mrs. Prouty works so hard for us. Ever since her husband died, she's always looking for ways to help us. She was telling me to come and stir some batter in the kitchen because nobody could help her like I do! She said I was like her own granddaughter. She even remembers the day I was born! Soon after I was born, Mama made soup for her and her husband—he was so sick then he couldn't eat anything else. Mama brought the soup to her house, and she was just about to say what happened while Mama was in her house, and then I interrupted her! I wanted to shrink down and hide in the batter! I couldn't help it; the words just flew out of my mouth. "Mrs. Prouty, your husband died ... what was that like?"

Mrs. Prouty got all nervous, and then tears started splashing out of her eyes and I got so scared ... how I wished I had never asked her! What was I thinking? Oh, Mama, if you'd been there to hear me you'd have gotten so mad at me. I wanted to get up and run away, but Mrs. Prouty just put her arm around me and wiped her tears on her sleeve. She said her husband dying wasn't as bad as she had imagined it would be, and that time has made it easier, and neighbors like us had helped! She brushed the hair back from my face and squeezed my shoulders, and then reminded me that I had interrupted her. She told me this long story about the day I was born. She told me that Mama was visiting her when she realized I was about to be born. Mrs. Prouty called Baba, and then helped Mama come back home before calling the midwife. I was born a few hours later! A week after I was born, Mama was already up and making soup for her!

Subhanallah, Buraq! Even then Mama never forgot to help us or her neighbors.

Then all of a sudden Mrs. Prouty grabbed the bowl I was stirring. "Come on," she said, "give me that batter, you are taking forever!" She started furiously scraping the batter into the pans and tossed them into the oven. Then she sat down and pulled me toward her. She said again that getting used to her husband dying was easier than she had thought it would be, and that she had lots of help. But my throat was turning into a big lump, Buraq. I just blurted out how scared I feel, and then I couldn't hold back my tears. She just said to go ahead and do it, and you know what? It really did feel good to just stop fighting with myself and let myself cry. And then the most astonishing words came out of my mouth. I was really shocked—I didn't even know I felt those things.

"I'm afraid Mama will die, and if she dies I will break into little pieces."

break...

into....

little....

pieces....

Did I say that?

I'm writing about this amazing time I had with Mrs. Prouty but when I write it, it seems so different from when it was actually happening. This is what she said to me—listen, Buraq, I think you will be amazed, and I think even though I was there to hear her say it, I just feel like I have to write it all down.

"You know, Nur, your mother might die, only God knows about that. But even if she does, and even if you do break, we are all around you and we will help. We will work together, and we will help each other, and we will make each other strong enough to face anything. Think of how many people have died since the world began. How many children have lost their parents? How many parents have lost their children? Here, my darling" (she said in the middle of it all), "do you want a tissue? This is the work of being human, Nur, and everybody everywhere has always had to do it. The important thing to remember is that even without love, people manage it, but you, you have so much love around you, and so much help. So try to think of those things when you feel scared. Here, Nur, I'll tell you a secret. Everything living ends in death. It is everywhere, in every person's life, but what makes every story different from the rest is how that person decides to deal with the pain of losing the one they love. Most people won't accept the pain, and that's too bad because it keeps them hiding in darkness. Here's the secret, my darling: Be different! Be strong! Don't fight the pain, but let it in, and you will see that it will transform itself into love and kindness, and you will see that you will soar through this like a butterfly!"

different   DiᵍᵍEᵣeʰ⁺
            butterfly ❀

STRONG

"Soar"

BREAK"

Pieces

Butterfly ✿

Thursday, July 10 | 08

Oh, Buraq, I just can't write. I need Grandma. I thought she would come, but she's having too much trouble walking.

What I was most afraid of has happened, Buraq. Mama has gone to Allah ... I just can't tell you about it now.... all I have for you is tears.

Friday, July 11 | 08

Today, Buraq, we buried Mama. But please forgive me if I can't write about it to you now. The house is full of people, and I must sit with them. And Yasemin, Hana, and Janine are coming with their moms.

Saturday, July 12 | 08

Subhanallah, Buraq, you won't believe what just happened! I was still in bed, waking up, and I had just remembered that Mama was gone and it felt so heavy and sad and I didn't even think I would be able to get up. Then I heard Mehmed calling my name from Mama's room. I ran to him. He was looking into the tank at the third monarch butterfly. The cocoon was hanging from the red cabbage leaf, and the butterfly was on the floor of the tank. Its body was thin and tight, and its wings were stretched right out and quivering.

"It's getting ready to fly! Quick! Go get Baba!"

But before Baba could get there, the butterfly flew up out of the tank and straight to Mama's pillow. It sat there quietly, fluttering its wings.

Baba smiled when he came into the room. Subhanallah! he said.

He threw open Mama's window, and the butterfly flew out. We all ran out onto the porch. We wanted to see where it would go first. It flew out over the garden, and we ran after it. It landed on the shortest sunflower.

I remembered the weak little shard of cocoon that was all the butterfly had left in the tank. I thought about Mama. By the time she went down into the grave, all that was left of her was just a dried-up shell, like the cocoon. Now she had wings! I knew then for the first time that she wasn't just with that shell of her we had left in the grave ... she was soaring somewhere, like this monarch butterfly! And what about her dream? She said she heard Muhammad, may Allah bless him and give him peace, tell her that I would have wings too! Could it really be? Could I really grow past all the pain and all the fear, and feel that I have wings? I almost thought I could hear Mama whispering to me, *Wait, habibti, wait. You will see. Allah is cherishing you.*

Sunday, July 13 | 08

Poor Mehmed. He crashed into the side of the house on his bike and snapped its front fender. His face is all scratched up. He just couldn't stop crying and saying how much he wanted Mama. Uncle Furqan and Baba sat with him and he finally fell asleep, crying, in Baba's arms. Later when he woke up Uncle Furqan told him a story from old India, "The Mustard Seed," about a woman whose little girl dies. She goes everywhere asking everyone for some medicine for her and finally comes to the home of the healer. He tells her he needs mustard seed to make the medicine and she says she will find it right away—mustard seed is easy to find. But he tells her it must be mustard seed that comes from a home where no one has ever died. She goes off carrying her dead child and expecting to find it right away, and does find it right away, except that when she checks to be sure no one has ever died in that house, she finds out that the grandfather has died. At the next house, it was the brother. At the next, the mother. Soon she has gone to every house, and sees that death has been everywhere. The old woman in the last house she visits says, "My dear, the dead are many, and the living are few." The mother begins to see that what she is living through was what Allah has planned for her. So, she lays her child in the grave and buries him, and returns to her family, wanting only to please Allah. Subhanallah, Buraq, we were all hanging on Uncle Furqan's words, but Mehmed was head over heels inside that story. And when it was finished and Mrs. Prouty had brought him a big scoop of blueberry ice cream, well, he was a different boy. Buraq, maybe I was a little bit different too. I remembered what Mrs. Prouty had been telling me about how everybody has to deal with death, but what makes a person different is how they choose to deal with the pain. Buraq, I want to do what she suggested! I want to be different. I want to be strong, and live a story full of light, not darkness and hiding. Death! You're not gonna ruin *this* Nur's life!

Monday, July 14 | 08

I walked through the house this morning before everyone got up and the silence really scared me. Mehmed woke up next, calling out for Mama. When I went into his room he just turned away from me and stuck his head under the covers. I felt so hurt, especially after last night. I ran back to my room and threw myself onto my settee. My throat was aching and I just started to cry and cry like I would never be able to stop. I didn't know how to be different, to be strong. It was all just a bunch of words, Buraq. I was remembering the butterfly on the sunflower, and the feeling that Mama was soaring away somewhere, and that I had wings beginning to grow, but none of that was real. It was just all my imagination! Why couldn't Mama just have beautiful wings in this life here with me? Why did she need to die? When I saw the butterfly fly away, I saw my mother and her beauty and her grace flying away from me. I wanted her here with me! I cried harder and harder and harder, but I began to see that no amount of crying would change anything, and finally I felt Baba sit on the floor beside the settee. "I'm here, Nur. I love you." Buraq, it was amazing. He didn't have to say anything—I just felt the pressure leave me slowly, and I actually started to feel peace come into my heart. Mehmed came in and crawled onto my bed, and we all just stayed there together, me and Mehmed on my bed, Baba on the floor, for a long time.

Then suddenly Baba jumped up. "Right!" he said. "Grab the grapefruits and let's go!"

"Where?" Mehmed asked.

"To the waterfall!"

It really helps to be in the woods, you know, Buraq?

The waterfall crashes,

Deafening,

And yet within the roar

There is silence.

This is what

Takes me into itself

And I go, leaving behind the sadness

That roars in me.

Then I remember

What Mama always said to me,

"Wait. You will see. Allah is cherishing you."

How does Baba know that bringing us to the waterfall is the best possible medicine? Even Mehmed was smiling by the time we got into the car to come back. In the afternoon Baba took us back to the cemetery. We lay down together on the grass near Mama's grave and Baba asked Allah to reach into our hearts and heal the wound that her death has inflicted on us.

Tuesday, July 15 | 08

Buraq, I did something really wrong today. I saw Baba's journal lying on his bed, and he wasn't home, and I opened it. I shouldn't have, and someday I will tell Baba and I pray he will forgive me ... but look what he wrote:

"Ya Firdaus, I never thought our time together would be so short, and what hurts the deepest is that when I turn to tell you how lovely your children are, I cannot. Nur has been so brave and gracious and appreciative of the support of our friends and family. She looks so like you, Firdaus, and you have passed your excellent character down to her. Mehmed is fierce and furious that you are gone. His path will be different—may Allah guide me as his father."

Wednesday, July 16 | 08

Today Mrs. Prouty and Auntie Ayshe went through Mama's closet and dresser and packed away her clothes. Mehmed threw a fit. He wanted them to leave everything alone. Finally Baba and Uncle Daoud came and took him to the waterfall. Poor kid. He just refuses to accept that Mama died. He insists she is coming back. It is so strange. He was with us at the cemetery, and Baba has been holding him and talking to him a lot, but he still insists. But you know, Buraq, now that I think about it, part of me feels the same way. I cannot tell you how many times I have stored away something inside my brain to tell Mama later. Well, how am I gonna tell her later? Oh, Buraq ...

Thursday, July 17 | 08

I just couldn't sit down and write out what happened last Thursday when Mama died, Buraq, I just didn't have the heart for it. But I want to tell you about it now. It happened at night. I think it was about 10:30. The house was full, but it was so quiet. In those last days Mama always wanted her door open. She knew people were coming to say goodbye so, even though she was in a lot of pain, she wanted anyone who wanted to, to come into her room and see her. Most of the time she had her eyes closed and her hands were still, but we knew she was awake because she was saying "Allah" all the time. But it didn't seem like a sound that came out of her mouth. It seemed to come from behind her breastbone, and when I heard it I felt like it was a hammer striking my heart like a big gong.

We were all there when it happened, Buraq. Uncle Furqan, Uncle Daoud, Auntie Sulma, Auntie Ayshe, Auntie Aliya, Yasemin, and dear Mrs. Prouty—they were standing around her bed. Baba and I were sitting on the bed with her. Her head was in Baba's lap and I was stroking her hair. She was facing Makkah. But Mehmed was sleeping in his room.

Uncle Daoud was reciting the Qur'an. Mama had become very quiet. I couldn't hear her prayers anymore, but I could still feel them in my heart. Baba was whispering to her.

"*La ilaha ill-Allah*"— there is no god but God—and "*Muhammadun rasul'Allah*"—Muhammad is His messenger.

We could see her lips moving, but there was no sound. When they stopped moving, she took one long breath. It came out of her as if riding on the word "A-l-l-a-h." Baba took hold of her suddenly. "Ya Firdaus, I didn't think you would go so soon!" He began to weep. My Uncle Daoud came and held onto him. Uncle asked Allah to make it easy for her, to make her grave as wide as the sky, and to make her able to answer the questions the angels would bring to her. He called out to her, just as if she were alive … but I am sure she heard because I have been taught the dead can hear. He reminded her when the angels come to her to answer that her Lord is Allah and that Muhammad is His messenger.

When Baba heard Uncle Daoud's voice, he sat up and stroked Mama's face and head.

My Auntie Ayshe came and held me in her arms. She was crying, and I started to cry. Mrs. Prouty came and kissed me. Yasemin and Auntie Aliya came to hug me. They were all crying too. And I am still crying. It's been a week now, the hardest week I ever lived through, and yet I have been in the company of so many people I love so much and who love me, and really, I am surprised to still be in one piece.

Right after *fajr* the next morning Baba let me watch while he washed Mama in a special way with soap and water he poured over her three times. At first I felt so scared I could hardly stand there, but something so strange happened ... I suddenly felt so peaceful, and so certain that I was in the right place at the right time. After that, everything seemed so important, as if it had been written to happen in exactly the way it had. And I knew that I would be with Mama again someday; I could see that nothing would ever break the connections between us, not even death.

Mama was covered with a big white sheet. Baba did everything under it so she never came uncovered. For the last washing he put rose oil in the water. Then he wrapped her body in a pure white cloth, round and round like a cocoon. Later I went near her and touched the cloth. The fragrance I had smelled in her room that other night was there again, but even stronger. It wasn't the rose oil smell—it was something else, but I could never put it into words what it was ...

Mehmed didn't want to come in, even though Baba encouraged him to. Later he wanted to know why we were washing her if she was already dead. Baba reminded us of the things he has told us so many times before ... that our lives are like moments, and our time in the grave will be much longer, and that time will end when Allah raises us up out of the grave to meet Him, and then we will understand the meaning of eternity. He said that's why this washing is so important and that Muhammad, may Allah bless him and give him peace, told his wife Aisha that if she died before he did, he would wash her and wrap her himself. And when his daughter Fatima died, her husband Ali washed her himself, may Allah be pleased with them all.

Friday, July 18 | 08

Friday again, already ... seven days Mama has been in the grave ... have we planted her? Will there be a sprout? Buraq, I just can't bring myself to go to the mosque today. I just want to be here in my room—I am finally ready to start telling you about what happened last week when we buried her.

We all went together to the mosque. I kept looking for her beside me and every time I remembered where she was I felt my heart break again. Yasemin and Auntie Aliya were with me and they helped me so much.

The mosque was packed! The men who couldn't get into the men's side had to pray out on the street, and the women who couldn't get into the women's side had to wait in the back garden.

After the Friday prayer, Baba stood up in front of everyone and what he said is etched in my heart.

"Oh Allah, this is Your slave Firdaus, daughter of Your slaves Abdallah and Halima. She has left this world and all the things she loved and will meet You in her grave.

She testified that there is no god but You alone, and that Muhammad is Your slave and messenger. She has left us to be with You, and You are the best to remain with. You know her better than we. Oh Allah, she is in need of Your mercy, please forgive her and have mercy on her. Please make her grave as wide as the sky and protect her until You raise her up to face her judgment. Please reward her for the way she worked to serve others, for the sacrifices she made for her family, for her fierce commitments to pleasing You."

After he finished talking, I got up and hugged him. Buraq, I cannot tell you how much I love my Baba! What he teaches me ... it just makes me feel so happy and safe.

I can still remember the first time I saw him cry. It was when Mama first got sick. I felt so scared when I saw that, Buraq. But you know, I remember him picking me up and kissing me then—I can still remember the feeling of his tears on my face. He was crying, but he loved me and was going to take care of me, and then it didn't feel scary anymore, because I could see that he was not afraid of what was happening or what he was feeling.

Sunday, July 20 | 08

It was a long ride to the cemetery, Buraq, when we went to bury Mama last week. The leaves glistened in the sunlight and the countryside seemed fresh and green. It seemed that there was a mile of cars following ours. When we got there, Baba, my uncles, and Yasemin's dad helped carry Mama's body to the place where the grave was. It was already dug, a big gaping hole in the ground. My uncles had come earlier to dig it. They put the body down. Then they stretched a big white cloth over the grave and four of Baba's friends held the corners. Yasemin and Auntie Aliya were standing with me, and I was keeping Mehmed close to me.

Baba jumped down into the grave under the covering. Then my uncles picked up Mama, and put her down into Baba's arms. He was talking to her and praying Allah would forgive her and be pleased with her, but I couldn't hear everything because of the cloth covering the grave. Soon my uncles helped him to climb out. They took away the cloth and we could see that he had laid Mama out with her cheek resting on a boulder. Then he took a handful of dirt and threw it into the grave saying, "Of this have We created you all."

Then he took a second handful and threw it in, saying, "To this We shall make you all return." On the third handful, he said, "And from it We shall bring you back again."

Baba cleaned his hands and came to hug Mehmed and me. He was crying, and so were we. My uncles and Uncle Uthman and some other friends of Baba's started to fill in the grave with their shovels. When it was all finished, Baba stood at the head of the grave and asked everyone to come close. He said, "Ya, Firdaus, daughter of Halima. Remember Islam, on which you left us. Remember there is no god but Allah, and that Muhammad is His slave and messenger. Remember that you have accepted Allah as your Lord, Islam as your religion, Muhammad as your Prophet, and the Qur'an as your Book. Remember these when the angels come to question you, *ya Firdaus!*"

We sat for a long time around her grave. Uncle Furqan, Uncle Daoud, Uncle Uthman, Baba, and some of his friends too were reciting the Qur'an. Then we left the cemetery as we had come, all together. The day was still bright and shining. When we got back home we found that our other neighbors had made food for us. We were all really hungry. We ate, and then we sat together and told stories about Mama. I always knew she had been kind and generous, but I never knew how much until I heard those stories! I think the most amazing one was from the nurses from the hospital who told us that when Mama was in hospital she would always find some way to go down the hall to visit some old lonely patient or another ... even when she was at her sickest, she was thinking of other people. Mashallah, she never even told us! We spent lots of time with her there but still she managed to do that without us ever seeing! And she gave Ms. Hanson, Ms. Jenkins, and Ms. Cardoon the most beautiful Turkish scarves. They said she was always friendly and very concerned about how others were feeling.

Monday, July 21 | 08

Today Uncle Daoud and Auntie Sulma had to go back to California, and Auntie Ayshe had to go back to Turkey. We didn't want them all to go back on the same day, but it had to be that way. I cried and cried when they went, it made everything seem so real, Buraq. Mehmed smashed his best truck with a rock. Later when Yasemin and Auntie Aliya came it seemed easier, and Mehmed got to go out with Baba, Uncle Furqan, and Uncle Uthman.

Tuesday, July 22 | 08

Oh, Buraq, the house is so empty, and now I just feel like I can't do anything. I just want to sleep or lie on my bed and cry. I miss Mama. I miss my grandma so much. We talk on the telephone but that just makes me miss her more, since I can't touch her or smell her.

Janine called me from her grandma's house in Palestine last night, but the connection wasn't very good so we couldn't talk too long. It seems like years until school starts. I wish I could call Mama—why is there no way to reach her, how can she possibly be so totally gone?

Wednesday, July 23 | 08

Our house is big and empty and stupid because my mother is not here anymore. Buraq, I just feel like I want to get away from the empty place she left and run away. Now I have to take care of my brother after Qur'an class until my father gets home from work. He's a good kid, Mehmed ... it's just that, well, we're not particularly interested in the same things. Except maybe books. I do love reading to him, and he is always so grateful. But it makes me crazy when his friends come over and they run me ragged. I just get everything straightened up and then turn around to find blocks scattered from wall to wall, a banana peel wrapped in a death-grip around the chair leg, and forty-seven limousines, pick-up trucks, Land Rovers, and tanks tangled up with socks, T-shirts, and jackets. He never would have dared to do that when Mama was here. She'd have skinned him alive. When I told him so he stormed out of the house.

Thursday, July 24 | 08

I am sitting on Mama's bed. It has been raining since early morning. Buraq, Mama has been gone for two weeks. At first everything was so new, and there was the light we all felt when she died, and the peace we felt at the grave, and the time with Uncle Daoud and Auntie Sulma and Auntie Ayshe ... but now they are all gone, and I can't feel the light anymore, and my heart aches. How can I live without her here? I just want her to be with me, I want her to sing sacred songs with me and tell me stories and brush my hair and make me a new blouse. Even if I say what she always said to me—*Wait. You will see. Allah is cherishing you. Wait. You will see. Allah is cherishing you. Wait. You will see. Allah is cherishing you*—over and over, the ache in my heart will not go away today.

Friday, July 25 | 08 – Black Friday

SO WHAT?

It's all very pretty,

This butterfly ditty

The chrysalis opens

The body shrinks

The wings expand.

But I say, "So what!?"

It really doesn't help

Not one bit...

You are gone, Mama, and the house is empty,

And your room is empty,

And my heart is empty.

Allah, I don't want to be ungrateful,

But when will it stop, this searing pain?

Saturday, July 26 | 08

Baba gave me a pair of letters my mother wrote to me. But I don't want to read them. Why couldn't she have given them to me herself? I'm just going to stash them in my trunk for now; I can't do anything else or I feel I might break.

He also gave me her quilt so I could have it on my bed. But I don't want it, Buraq. I don't even want to look at it again. You know, I know it sounds silly, but I really wanted that quilt to make her better, and it didn't. That's why I don't want to look at it again. I just stuffed it into my closet.

I still have to hang up all the laundry. Mrs. Prouty said she would help me, but I know she isn't feeling well, so I don't want to ask her. Mehmed is being a monster and refusing to clean his room again and pick up his things from the living room. Baba has told me to just pick up what he leaves around the house outside his room, but even that's a huge job! Today I was lugging a huge basket of wet sheets across the living-room floor and I tripped over one of his tractors in the middle of the floor. And he had the nerve to blame me for breaking it! Finally Baba decided to punish him: He has to pay the price of the tractor ... to me!!

Sunday, July 27 | 08

Yasemin called and invited me to come over and bring
Mehmed too. Her brothers were going fishing and they
could take him. Baba gave his permission and we went over
in the morning. Mehmed was really excited! He ended up
catching a big perch that they cooked and ate on the beach.
Auntie Aliya and Yasemin and I made *manti*, little dumplings
of dough and meat. I am amazed at how much Yasemin has
been practicing her pastry rolling. I haven't seen her do it
since last year. She flings that rolling rod around so skillfully,
and the pastry turns into fine silk before your very eyes ...
then we cut it into little squares and put a tiny bit of spiced
meat in the middle of each square and squeeze the corners
so when they are boiled they won't fall apart. Auntie Aliya
showed us a different way to make manti too. She rolled
out a circle of dough, covered it all over with spicy ground
meat and then rolled it up into a log. Then she wrapped the
log in a piece of muslin, a really thin cotton cloth, brought
the ends of the log together and tied the floppy cloth ends
together, and plopped it in the boiling water. After it had
boiled for a while she took it out, untied it, rolled it out of
the cloth, and sliced it into pinwheels. These she put on a

plate, poured garlic yogurt over and then spicy red-pepper oil, and—yummmm!—it was so good.

But do you know what, Buraq, as much as I loved being there with Yasemin and Auntie Aliya, and especially doing all that cooking, it just doesn't feel right without Mama. She was always there, talking and laughing with Auntie Aliya and remembering things they saw together in Turkey. I don't want to go there again, it makes it hurt too much, it makes me miss Mama too much!

Monday, July 28 | 08

Baba said I can go to camp, Buraq! Allah answered my
prayers after all! When I got *that flyer* from school last fall
I was sure he would never let me go. That camp belongs
to the wife of Baba's friend at work, can you believe it? It is
a camp only for girls, and there are no men even working
there. And, they have horses! I am going two weeks on
Sunday, and Mrs. Prouty is going to take me shopping for
some new clothes I need. Mehmed will stay with her while
I am gone.

Tuesday, July 29 | 08

This morning Mehmed found a chrysalis on his own! He was so excited. He was running in the field next door, and he saw it hanging on a chokecherry bush right in front of him. I realized when I saw his excitement how much he has changed since Mama died. He used to get excited about a lot more things ... seeing him with his very own chrysalis was like seeing the old Mehmed, thank heavens! He set up one of the tanks in his room for it. He had broken the branch very carefully and he was able to prop it up inside the tank. Then we looked through some pictures of caterpillars. He is determined to find one at that stage and have it spin its cocoon inside his tank from the inside of the top screen.

It happened again, Buraq, I just wanted to run and tell Mama that Mehmed is doing better. How? Where am I supposed to find her?

Wednesday, July 30 | 08

This morning Mrs. Prouty and I went to buy some clothes for me to take to camp. I got some lightweight running shoes. I wore them home—I felt so light! I needed a thin fleece jacket to wear at night and some sports pants that go past my knees for games and swimming, and we found some really nice cool tops that are actually long enough not to leave my belly sticking out. Mama, where are you, how can I ask you if these things we bought are OK? You always knew what would suit me and what wouldn't.

Thursday, July 31 | 08

Uncle Furqan is coming over to eat (Baba is making his famous hamburgers on home-made buns) and then we are going to the waterfall. I haven't seen Uncle in a while.

Friday, August 1 | 08

I wanted to write last night and tell you about the waterfall but we came in really late because we stayed there past sunset. We prayed *maghrib* and *isha* out there. Baba and Uncle Furqan built a fire on the rocks. Uncle Furqan brought marshmallows and chocolate and graham crackers and we made s'mores! He didn't tell us until the fire was roaring and then he just brought them out! The best part was when Baba told us the story of a very special picnic he had with Mama. He said she had begged him to bring her to that very waterfall one late afternoon. They sat eating fried chicken and cucumbers and she told him she was pregnant ... with me! Of course, Mehmed wanted to know immediately where she told Baba when he was coming. He was so disappointed to hear it was only in the living room!

But he perked up when he heard that when Baba found out she was carrying a boy, he picked her up and spun her around! Uncle Furqan jokingly asked Mehmed if he remembered, and Mehmed said, "Of course! I just wanted to see if he remembered!" Mama, his sense of humor is finally coming back.

Saturday, August 2 | 08

A group of monarch butterflies is called a rabble! Hilarious! Who makes these things up, anyway? Some people also say a rainbow of butterflies or, better yet, a kaleidoscope of butterflies. Definitely more poetic.

A kaleidoscope of butterflies
spilled across the furry milkweed
and was gone
in an instant
like Mama.

Sunday, August 3 | 08

Only a week until I go to camp! I know it sounds selfish,
Buraq, but I can't wait to go. You know why? I never went
to camp before. That is, Mama never sent me to camp, we
never talked about going to camp, so I'm going somewhere
new, somewhere I've never been while she was in my life. So
maybe that means I won't have memories to hurt my heart.

Monday, August 4 | 08

Today I had to go to the doctor to get a physical for camp. It was the same building that Mama's first doctor was in. I wanted to get a different doctor, I didn't want to go anywhere near that building, but Baba insisted we just get it over with and get home. He forgot to bring my immunization record so we had to go home and then back again!

Wednesday, August 6 | 08

Mehmed has been really strange lately. Honestly, sometimes I think he's doing better and then sometimes it all falls out the window and he seems worse than ever. He yelled at me today and threw his math book at me when I asked him to sit down and show me his homework. Baba suggested that if he does that again I should tell him I see he is angry and ask him if he needs anything from me. He said Mehmed is just beginning to realize Mama is not coming back, that's probably why he is doing things like this. It is hard to be patient, and sometimes I'd like to throw my whole room at somebody, because I've known for a long time that she's not coming back.

Sunday, August 10 | 08

Buraq, I really wanted to come to this camp but now that I am here I feel like a square peg in a round hole. I feel really lonely. There's not a single covered girl here except for me, and the other girls, even though they try to be nice to me, keep their distance. You know, for the first time I wondered what would happen if I just decided to be like everyone else and uncover my head. It would be so freeing: Nobody would think I was different, maybe nobody would even ask about my religion!

After dinner we had a long hike up to one of the upper meadows. We played some games while the counselors built a big campfire. Oh, it smelled so good, Burak, I love the smell of wood smoke. We sat around it and sang songs and I suddenly felt so lonely for Mama, and for Baba and Mehmed and Uncle Furqan, for the *illahis*, the sacred songs Mama used to sing. I tried to share one but it didn't seem like anyone was particularly interested, so I just gave up. I can really see how different my life has been to that of the other girls here. And when I try to share what I have learned, they just don't seem interested. How can I communicate with them?

Monday, August 11 | 08

The counselor in our cabin is Sandra. I set my clock so I could pray *fajr* and she got really mad at me for disturbing the other girls. She says I can't get up early like that, no way. I tried to tell her that I can't *not* get up, but she wouldn't listen to me. I'm going to try and talk to the camp director; they say she is really nice.

Tuesday, August 12 | 08

Canoeing! We had to learn how to bounce the half-sunk canoe from side to side to wash most of the water out of it! It was a blast. The only thing was, the girls were all talking so much and making so much noise. I remember canoeing with Uncle Furqan and what was so amazing was the *silence*. The canoe makes almost no noise going through the water, except for just a few drips and sloshes from the paddles when you lift them out of the water. In this crowd of girls, nobody seemed interested in silence.

The camp director really is nice. She said it's OK for me to get up for *fajr*. I am so glad, because this morning I had to miss it or Sandra would have skinned me alive. All day long I have carried this sadness in my heart and I am so glad I won't have to miss it again. It is one of my favorite parts of the day.

But unfortunately *fajr* isn't the only problem. Tonight I had to leave the dining hall early so I could wash and pray *maghrib* and I forgot to tell Sandra. She was so mad at me. Some of my cabin mates seemed like they were beginning to warm up to me, but this really seemed to set them back. And I heard them whispering that my mother died. My throat got coiled up so tight I thought I would explode.

Wednesday, August 13 | 08

Buraq, I had a terrible dream. I am writing with my flashlight in the middle of the night and I'm shaking. I dreamed of Mama, Buraq, but she didn't look happy, she looked so scared and weak. She asked me where my brother was. I want to go home, Buraq. I love the horses and the canoes and everything but I need to go home and help Baba and Mehmed. It isn't right for me to be out here trying to have a good time while they are at home without me. It is hard enough for them to be without Mama.

Today I am going to the camp director to ask her to call Baba to come and get me.

Thursday, August 14 | 08

Baba was there in one hour! I was worried he would be mad at me, but he wasn't. He was so kind and patient and on the way home we bought some sandwiches and fruit and then we hiked up to the waterfall.

Baba smiled and asked me, "What is wrong, my dear Nur?"

I turned my head away. I enjoyed time with Baba and all, but I wanted to face in the other direction, toward the horizon, and be in my own world ... a world where my sadness would be carried off by my beautiful butterflies ... away from me ... and maybe they would even carry Mama back to me.

I could hear Baba's breath, it seemed heavy. Then he said that when Mama died her face was calm. He said he was in so much pain. I never really thought about his pain. But he said when he looks back now, he feels there was so much light in the room. He says it seems now that he could feel the presence of happiness there, and a deep hope that things would be OK. He said sometimes he thinks of the Prophet sitting alone in the utter darkness of the Cave of

Hira, when suddenly it was filled with light, and the Angel Jibril was there. Baba said he wondered if the Prophet at that moment, in spite of the tremendous fear that he felt, also felt peace, and reassurance? It seemed to Baba that he must have ... at least, that is what Baba says *he* felt in that moment when his whole world was changing. He remembers weeping and fighting against things with all his might, and yet he felt peace within that. He said he knew for sure that everything that was happening had a meaning behind it.

His voice trailed away, as if he had just noticed that I was still staring off at the horizon. I didn't want to be mean; I just felt that if I looked away from the horizon I would break into a thousand teardrops splashing over the mossy rocks and crashing down the falls. I reached behind me and put my hand on his knee.

"You will heal, Nuri," he said. "Trust me. You will come to see that Allah does not make mistakes."

I kept looking toward the horizon. I thought, "If only my butterflies could carry the sadness away, Mama could return ... if there's no sadness, Mama could come back for sure! Because everything is happier with Mama."

Baba's voice brought me back. "Nur, Mama's death was the start of a new beginning."

I thought to myself, still hoping Mama could come from the horizon ... what was Baba talking about? What does Mama's death have to do with the Prophet in the Cave of Hira? Mama's death brought sadness and misery—how was she happy? How can I be happy??

I turned to Baba and smiled. I just wanted to hide my sadness and misery from him. He was trying so hard, but for some reason I couldn't let him in.

Eventually, we hiked back out of the woods, and got in the car, and drove and drove, for so long it felt like forever ... this pain feels like forever...

Friday, August 15 | 08

When Mehmed saw me this morning, he came running and buried his face in my tummy! He was so sweet, you would hardly believe he was the same boy I left, who was throwing his books at me instead of putting them in the bookcase. I noticed, by the way, that his room was really neat. When I asked him about it he said Mrs. Prouty had straightened it up. But then he really surprised me—he said he was sorry for throwing the books. Mashallah, Mehmed, mashallah! But I noticed in his room that the chrysalis tank was empty and open. I asked him what had happened. Buraq, his lip started to tremble, and there were tears in his eyes ... something went wrong with the chrysalis ... he said it turned black, like they always do, and then he could see the butterfly's folded wings inside. When it opened there was only one wing and the body was misshapen. After it came out it was still and lifeless, and finally he and Baba decided to leave it out in the field. He hasn't felt like going out and looking for any new ones. Later I saw he'd taken the tank and put it in the garage. Poor kid. I just wanted to crawl into my bed and disappear. What was I thinking, trying to leave him and go to camp?

Tuesday, August 26 | 08

Baba told me a story today. But he told me as if he were an old man. He changed his voice and that made his face seem really old! He introduced himself as Wahid, the perfume-maker. He lived in Kolkata in India. He said there was a man who, on his trips to buy rose oil, would always come and stay with him. They grew to like each other and looked forward to being together. But Wahid noticed that the man always seemed a little sad. So one day after they had gotten to know each other better, he asked him why. The man said he was in love with his wife, and he missed her when he went away.

Well, one day his friend arrived after a long absence, and within an hour or two Wahid noticed something different about him. He seemed more at ease. He asked him why. The man said the strangest thing. He said his wife had died.

"But how would that make you feel more at ease?" Wahid asked.

"Well," said the man, "before when I went away, I always had to leave her behind, at home alone. But this time, subhanallah. I wasn't leaving her at home, because she's not there anymore, and when I set off I realized that it felt as though she was traveling with me." He patted his heart. "I really feel like she's here with me!"

Don't get me wrong, Buraq, I really loved watching Baba play the part of somebody else. Every time we fool around like that I feel so happy. I can still remember, two years ago when she first found out she was sick, he played a crazy doctor and Mama played the part of a very weak, sick lady who could barely walk, going into his clinic (my desk in my bedroom). We were all so afraid of what the doctors were saying, so we decided to rewrite the story right then and there. We were all laughing and soon we were crying and hugging too but somehow we all felt so much better after. Well, this time I didn't feel better afterwards. I just felt confused. I loved watching and listening to Baba, but I hated his dumb story! My Mama died and I am NOT satisfied to carry her around "here." OK, Buraq, I know that sometimes it seems Grandma is "here" with me, sometimes I can almost hear the sound of her voice and feel the touch of her hands, but that is so different. I am used to Grandma being someplace else. But Mama was always here, and always took care of me. I feel so afraid, Buraq. What will I do without Mama?

Wednesday, August 27 | 08

Today was Mehmed's birthday; he turned seven. Mashallah, rather than giving him a chance to just think, *Me, me, me, my birthday*, Baba took him to the homeless shelter to hand out cupcakes and chocolate. Then they made loads of pizza together and we took him with his friends to the waterfall for a picnic. He had a good day but he fell apart after we got home. He yelled at Baba when he told him to put his bike away. When Baba took his arm and held him close and reminded him about his manners, he burst into tears and cried for almost 15 minutes. Baba just held onto him the whole time and finally Mehmed said, "Why did Allah have to take my mother? Every kid I know has a mama, why did He have to take mine?" Baba told him they would go back to the waterfall in the moonlight and pray the Prayer of Need so that Allah would make him feel better.

Can you imagine how awful it would have been if I had been stuck away at camp and had missed Mehmed's birthday? And especially the moonlight trip to the waterfall? I shudder to think about it.

The waterfall was magical, Buraq. The moon was so bright

and the waterfall looked like molten silver. We prayed the night prayer, and then we all prayed the Prayer of Need together. We even went in the pool. When we were driving home Mehmed fell asleep on my lap and everything seemed so much easier. But I still feel such an ache in my heart that I can't tell Mama these things. Do you think she knows anyway, Buraq?

Thursday, August 28 | 08

Today Uncle Furqan is coming to get us in his other car, his big red rig, and take us up to Sauble Beach! He knows a really quiet place so we can be away from the crowds and even sleep on the beach.

Ramadan starts in three days' time! Yikes, it seems like the last Ramadan was just a few months ago. Mama was so sick last Ramadan, but still we all thought for sure she was going to get better.

I'm nervous, Buraq ... how will I manage everything this year without Mama? How can we get up in the night to eat when she is not there? And who will cook our evening food? Who will tell us special stories? Who will encourage me to read though the Qur'an? Who will go with me to taraweeh, the twenty repetitions of the prayer?

Friday, August 29 | 08

We've pitched a tent right at the edge of the woods on a little pebble beach and there's nobody in sight. We stayed up by the fire and then let it go out so we could watch the sky, and saw a couple of shooting stars. This morning we made pancakes and eggs on Uncle Furqan's camp stove. Yum! Mehmed was happier than I have seen him for a long time. Dear Mama, I think you would have been relieved—I know I was. Mama, I'll always remember how much you loved being on the beach. I thought about you all the time the sun was setting out over the lake last night. Everything turned the most amazing crimson in the last few minutes, and then the sun was gone … like you, Mama. Gone. I miss you so much.

Saturday, August 30 | 08

Oh, the morning was glorious! We just stayed up after *fajr* and watched the sun rise. Before breakfast we hiked around in the woods for a while, and after breakfast we had a long lazy swim. We jumped in the car right after the noon prayer, stopped on the way home to buy things we need in the kitchen for Ramadan, and got home just in time to pray the afternoon prayer. Mehmed and I hung up the Ramadan lights and two Moroccan lanterns in the kitchen and Mrs. Prouty came to bake the Turkish breads *pogaca*, *simit* and *acma* for us to put in the freezer for *sahurs*, the pre-dawn breakfasts. She wanted me to help her, and take notes so I can write down the recipes and directions.

I remember last Ramadan Mama had just had another round of her chemo and was so sick ... but she insisted on sitting in the rocker and telling Mrs. Prouty every single thing she had to do to make the little breads. Ramadan just wouldn't be Ramadan without them stuffed in the freezer. At least not in our house anyway. I know it's the same in Yasemin's house. Her mother rolls out pastry dough like silk. Her family came from near Izmir and they know so many varieties of *borek* it'll make your head spin ... rolled, folded, pleated, pinched, baked, boiled, fried, the list is endless.

At night we did the first *taraweeh* prayer out in the garden. I was a little worried it would seem long but Uncle Furqan's recitations are so clear it was easy to get lost in the sounds of the Qur'an and then the time really flew by. That's how it is in Ramadan, you know, Buraq? Subhanallah, Allah makes it all seem so easy...

Sunday, August 31 | 08

The first day of Ramadan. I was worrying about how hard it would be without Mama at sahur and, it was true, I really did miss her. When I told Baba, he asked me to remember how much pain she was in last Ramadan... That pain is over for her, alhamdulillah.

Monday, September 1 | 08

I really am grateful that Mama is no longer in pain but I miss her so much and it is much harder now in Ramadan. I never realized how much she did for us. She would always make us our favorite foods to eat after the evening prayer when we have our first meal of the day. She would sit with us in that last hour before we broke our fast, the hour that always seemed like it might last a whole day. She would tell us stories of the prophets, peace upon them all, and of the companions of the Prophet Muhammad, may Allah bless him and give him peace. I miss her. I want her to come back and tell me stories. I want her to come and make me sweet apricots and cream. I can't do all this work myself! I am angry, and so sad. I just cried and cried in *taraweeh* tonight because I see that one of the things I miss most is Mama's love of Muhammad. When she was telling me about him, I always felt like he had just been here, like I could almost remember the sound of his voice or something. Now it all feels so far away.

And I hate going to school without seeing her. How can I know if I have my clothes on right? She always helped me choose the right color scarf. She always told me if my skirt wasn't straight or if my top was too wrinkled.

Anyway, Buraq, today was the first day of school and another really sad thing is that our science teacher Mr. Jameson is not there anymore; he has gone to Ottawa. Janine isn't back yet, not till next week. But I saw Hana, Yasemin, and Chloe. They all had amazing stories to tell about their summer trips. I didn't have too much to say, just sat and listened. It's a good thing too because I'm sure if I had started talking I would have ended up crying.

Friday, September 5 | 08

It's been five days since I've written to you, Buraq! Ramadan is so busy. With school and *taraweeh* every night it is hard to fit everything in. It is so nice having Uncle Furqan here, alhamdulillah. He says he might stay right through Ramadan. I hope he does, because it is soooo hard without Mama. It's easier when he is here, and he's a great cook too!

Monday, May 3 | 10

Dear Buraq, it's me, Nur, hoping and praying that you will forgive me for my long silence. You will, won't you? Even though I left you alone and neglected on the shelf for a whole year and a half? It was Ramadan when I was writing last, and then it was time to celebrate Eid ... my life just ran away from me. Well, that is only partly true ... as I look back I can see that as much as I love you, dear Buraq, I needed a break! I was always writing to you about Mama, and suddenly I just couldn't do it anymore. I couldn't think about it or read about it or talk about it.

Ramadan and Eid were so hard. School was starting again ... right from the very beginning I had so much homework. I was responsible for helping Mehmed after school and lots of days I had to help cook too. Mrs. Prouty was helping a lot, but then she got sick and went to stay with her daughter in Minnesota. That felt like a major earthquake and made me feel as though Mama had just died, all over again. I think I cried every single day for two weeks. Mehmed had a dreadful time at school, his teacher was calling Baba every other day complaining about him. That really made me mad. I had plenty of complaints about him from the times when I was responsible for him, but I never forgot why he was behaving so badly, poor kid. It seems like Baba and Uncle Furqan were the only ones who could deal with him. Then Baba got a new job, teaching writing online. That meant he didn't have to go out to work every day anymore. He moved out of the room he'd shared with Mama and into a smaller one downstairs, and then he made his office in Mama's room. It's really nice—sometimes he works on the balcony, and the best part of all is that now he's home when we get home from school. This has made such a big difference for Mehmed, Buraq. Almost overnight he stopped throwing tantrums with me, and within two weeks his teacher called to say how much better he was doing at school. It seemed like when Mrs. Prouty left he just fell apart, it was all just too much.

So anyway, everything was much easier then. Near the end of the year I had a dream about Mama! I saw Mama, Buraq! It was sooo clear, you wouldn't believe it. She came to put some things away in my closet. I heard something in there, and I opened the door and there she was. And do you know what? The walls of my closet were gone! There was no end to it, it stretched out and out and out, who knows how far, and it was filled with the most beautiful fabric folded in neat piles, amazing bright colors, and then there were baskets, the most amazing shapes and colors, and some were filled with green emeralds, brilliant red rubies, deep blue lapis lazuli, shining sapphires, and glittering diamonds, and others were filled with golden bracelets, rings, and necklaces. When I saw Mama, she was folding her quilt! She asked me in the dream if I had read her letters. I said no, I hadn't read them, because I felt that if I didn't read them it wouldn't be true that she was dead. She just smiled at me and then I woke up ... it finally made sense, Buraq! I suddenly could understand what Baba was saying about what the Prophet might have felt when he was in the Cave of Hira, when the Angel Jibril brought light into the cave. All those things Baba said to me that day at the waterfall made sense, about the peace that seems hidden inside the pain, about everything that happens having a meaning behind it, about Allah not making mistakes—it all made sense, Buraq! Subhanallah, Baba is really amazing. I see now that the light and happiness of Mama was always with her, and continues to surround me ... whether she was going through a terrible time or has now passed ... no one can take that light away, because it's in a safe place in our hearts. Mama's happiness is in my heart, and continues to thrive. Even when she was on her deathbed, she continued to possess that light. It's like these butterflies, all concealed in their dark cocoons. Even though I can't see them, I know what's inside is radiant. Ha ha! I can't help but laughing at myself! Laughing at my ignorance! Baba was right all along!

During Mama's death there would have been so much light, because Mama was filled with light. That's what my dream was about! Oh Allah! How merciful you are!

OK, gotta go, Baba has started the car!

Buraq, last night I finally opened Mama's letters. There was a note on one of them: "Read me first."

Dearest Nur,

Today as I write this letter, you have gone off with Mehmed to search for monarch cocoons. I am so amazed at how Allah plans things. I never dreamed I would ever get sick like this, and I was sure at the start that I would be able to find a way to get better. Maybe I still will, but it is so much harder than I ever thought. So I have been beginning to think about the possibility that you might have to grow up without me, and that set me to remembering another girl we both know and love so much who lost her mother when she was around fifteen years old. Before I start, I want you to remember how fortunate you are to be living in a time and place of peace, for all over the world in all times everyone has not had the opportunity to live that way, habibti. And sometimes the ones who were closest to Allah suffered the most ... a thing we can hardly even imagine in our world, yet we must, and we must be willing to give our lives if Allah wants them, for they are His, not ours.

Do you remember how the Qurayshi people in Makkah wanted to do whatever they could to stop the Prophet Muhammad telling them about Allah? They just didn't want to hear it, to hear anything that would lead them to change their lives.

Finally they told Muhammad's clansman that if they didn't stop him telling people about Islam, nobody could marry their daughters or sons, and none of them could buy or sell anything! They wrote it up on a piece of calfskin and hung it inside the Kaaba. The Prophet's clan decided they should live together in the same part of Makkah, away from all the houses and shops. For two years, some say even longer, they couldn't buy food or supplies. They had some friends who would bring sacks of rice and other things to them, but after months went by it started getting harder and harder. It is said that the whole thing was so hard on the Prophet's wife, Khadija, that she died a little while after it was over.

When she died, who was about your age? Her daughter Fatima! There seem to have been very few details written about those days, but there is a lot written about how, after her mother died, Fatima redoubled her efforts to support her father in his work, so much so that soon they started calling her "the mother of her father." She was known for her generosity, and so, I pray, my dearest Nur, will you be. Be patient, and then more patient, and then again more patient, until you can see the wisdom in all that Allah decrees. I love you, my dearest Nur, and I am so grateful to have a daughter to whom I can write such a letter, knowing full well that you will understand and live by it.

Love, annen, your Mama

Oh, Buraq, I'm afraid I don't know how to be that patient.

Wednesday, May 5 | 10

Another letter, Buraq. This one made me cry, but every time I reread it I feel better. Maybe everything will be OK after all.

Dearest Nur,

Thank you so much for this quilt. I am so touched that you had the idea, and that you used your money to buy something that would make me more comfortable. Well, I can assure you, my dear, that it certainly does make me more comfortable. You know how I feel about lavenders and blues. The lavenders and blues of this quilt are so restful to my tired spirit, and the pinks and greens with them refresh me and cheer me up. I love the intricate designs. I never get tired of looking at the little diamond starbursts and the borders of leaves and stems. Do you remember the quilt we made with Grandma when we visited her in Istanbul? You were only seven then, dear Nur, but, mashallah, your stitching was as straight and true as your little heart. May Allah always make you straight and true in all that you do. I have great faith that Allah is guiding you for some special purpose, my dear, and that everything that happens in your life, including something so dire as your mother dying, will be for your benefit. You must never forget that in the days ahead, when the wretched devil will want you to forget and will whisper to you to rebel and complain against what Allah has destined for you. He can convince us of all kinds of things and when we listen to him we can become angry and resentful and full of self-pity, all of which dissolves our gratitude. So may your Guardian Lord Allah guide your every step and protect you from the wiles of the devil.

Love, Mama

Thursday, May 6 | 10

Today Hana and Yasemin came over after school. I showed them Mama's letter. The first thing Hana said was, "Her name was *Annen*? I thought it was Firdaus." I had to explain to them that *annen* is the Turkish for "your mother" and it is pronounced *an-yen*. And that sometimes I call her Annem, which means my mother. And that I sometimes call Grandma Anannem. They read the letter together, and they both cried, Buraq. They said it was the most beautiful thing they had ever read. Then they wanted to see another one so I showed them the one about Fatima, the Prophet's daughter. Hana said, "I never knew they were treated so badly. I can't think of anything I believe so much that I'd be willing to go out and live in the bushes for it." Even though I felt grateful that they could see something of Mama's beauty in the letters, still, when they left I felt heavy thinking of them each going home to their mothers while I am here in this house without mine. As much as I sometimes feel her, I still can't touch her, or smell her, or hear her voice! That empty place makes me want to scream!

We are getting ready to go to Istanbul, Buraq! I am so excited. Baba promised Mama that he would do all he could to help us feel connected to Grandma and Auntie Ayshe and our other Turkish friends there. That promise makes me really happy. I am glad my mother was Turkish. I think Turkish people are really interesting. They are so careful about many things. Like their food, for instance. Everything they do with food is amazing. No just throwing things into a pot any old way for them. Things are rolled, stuffed, twisted, nested, layered … their recipes are really artistic.

And come to think of it, their art is really amazing … like marbling. Yasemin's mother helped us do that. It was so amazing, how the colors just float on the surface of the liquid, and then stick to the paper when you lay it on top. And the colors only stick to the paper because they have added—get this, Buraq—the *gall* from an ox to the paint! Amazing!

Buraq, it's the middle of the night and I can't get back to sleep!

I am weaving this heart-basket
With rushes from the river of tears.
I am weaving it broad, and deep, and empty.
And will gladly bear
The weight of its fullness.

What a strange little poem! I hardly understand it—it just sort of flowed from my pen.

I have missed Grandma so much. I can't wait to just curl up next to her and smell her. She always smells like lavender because she keeps huge bundles of it all over her house. My grandfather planted it for her in her garden the year they moved to their little house in Fatih. I remember because that's the year we visited. It was a little clump in the corner of her yard. Then Uncle Furqan went to visit a few years later and brought back a photo ... the whole garden was full of lavender!

Lavender! That's it! I need to sniff my lavender sachet and then I can probably get back to sleep. G'night, Buraq!

Friday, May 7 | 10

Today, after Friday prayer, Baba took me and Mehmed for a hike. I know it's too early for chrysalises, but I miss seeing them. It's been a long winter so I couldn't help but look for them anyway. But, oh, the trilliums, the deep reds and the whites! Poor Mehmed, he wanted so badly to pick them. I told him if he did they'd be dead in a few hours but here they will live for much longer. I was really struck by how he reacted to my advice. He actually listened. I think he is thriving from having Baba around more.

Saturday, May 8 | 10

I have more work for my exams than I thought I had, and this morning in Qur'an class I found out I have to recite all of the eighth section next week. Yikes! I guess I'll be a prisoner in my room for a while. At least I know we leave for Istanbul on June 10! Alhamdulillah. For once I won't be the only one left behind at the annual end-of-school exodus. Chloe nearly fell off her chair when I told her we were going. And we're leaving before her! So for once she can say goodbye to me!

Sunday, May 16 | 10

Today I started memorizing part seven of the Qur'an. After that, I'll have six more, and then I'll be an *Hafiza-Qur'an*, one who has memorized it all! I like to think of myself walking around with the whole Qur'an in me. I remember back when I started memorizing it ... I was only about four, and I didn't even know what was happening to me. Mama would take me to the apple orchard down the road and I would visit each tree and recite one short chapter from memory. Before I understood what the words meant, I could recite my way through half of the last section; that's 36 chapters! Mostly they are short ones, many only one page. Now somehow it is harder. Some of the chapters are very long and much harder to memorize. But there is one thing I can understand that I couldn't really see before, and that's that if the Qur'an is really living inside many people, instead of just sitting over there on the shelf, it will actually be able to help us much more. It isn't like an ordinary book, full of information that you can get to the bottom of. It is a living being.

Mehmed has memorized the last three parts ... he has a memory like a computer, subhanallah! His teacher says he is brilliant.

Thursday, June 10 | 10 *Morning*

Buraq, we're on the way to the airport. Mehmed and I are sitting in the back seat of Uncle Furqan's car and Baba's with him in the front. Mehmed has his nose stuck in a book he picked up from school about the ancient Egyptians. You'd think he was a regular world traveler. He just can't tear himself away from the mummies tombs, I guess.

I am so excited. Janine, Hana, and Yasemin came over to say goodbye. That was a great change! Usually I am the one going to say goodbye to *them*.

Thursday, June 10 | 10 Evening

There is the cutest baby in the seat in front of us. He smiles and snuggles one minute, and the next he goes into a rage because he can't crawl around on the floor. I took him for a little walk to the back of the plane. I kept him happy for a while with some apple slices I brought with me, and that made me feel easier and more comfortable. When I came back to sit down again, Baba leaned over to me and whispered, "Nur, my darling, you are so like your mother, somehow never quite happy unless you are helping someone." Well, I was sure for a moment that I was flying that plane with my heart, not the other way around. I love my Baba!

Friday, June 11 | 10

We're here, Buraq! I cannot believe how much Istanbul has changed since we came before, six years ago. It is sparkly here! There are so many new buildings, and so many trees! There are trees everywhere! From the plane we could see the incredible blue-gleaming Bosphorus and the Topkapi Palace sprawling over the hillside. I just got chills all over me when I saw it ... from within those walls millions of people were governed and guarded and protected, to live good lives, as so few other people had ever been, for over eight hundred years!

Mama's cousin, Uncle Hasan, picked us up from the airport and when we got down into the parking garage and into the car, there was Grandma! She still has so much trouble walking now, even though she is much better than she was two years ago. She insisted and insisted they bring her to the airport anyway. Her hair is whiter and thinner than it was, but she has such bright eyes and soft skin. Her face is still beautiful. She really hasn't changed that much, except for her difficulty walking.

Buraq, I don't know how it happened but the moment I looked into her eyes it was as though Mama had just died! We all just burst out crying. Why? Even Baba couldn't even talk for ten minutes. We all just sat there in the car in the parking garage, holding onto each other and crying. Somehow it seemed like this was why we had to come. Somehow a piece of our work had been hanging unfinished, and we didn't even realize it. Well, maybe Baba did, but I didn't. Maybe that's even why Mama wanted us to come.

Finally Uncle Hasan drove us to Fatih. The traffic on the big highways was terrible and it took us ages. But when we turned into the little narrow street where Grandma's house is, I was surprised by how quiet it was, and how much I remembered it. Part of the street is lined by the huge walls of the Fatih Mosque Complex, and on the other side of the street there is a huge old stone building that used to house a great madrasah. Uncle Hasan's friend Mahmoud is starting up a new Qur'an school there now.

When we got to Grandma's house and saw Auntie Ayshe it started all over again, because the last time we saw her was after Mama's funeral. Grandma made us tell her all about Mama's last days, how it was for her when she died, and how the burial was. She had heard it all before over the telephone, but it's the telling that matters, isn't it? I know she was really upset that she couldn't make the trip.

I felt a lot of comfort afterwards, even though we cried a lot—something felt lighter in me.

Buraq, the *adhan*! The call to prayer. I can hear it from about ten different mosques, in ten different voices, in ten different tunes, all around me. It is so beautiful, subhanallah! I remember Auntie Ayshe telling me when she was visiting us that the *adhan* is one thing she would hate to live without. She told me how the Russians destroyed the mosques in Sofia, Bulgaria in 1878, all of them on the same night with dynamite during a thunderstorm, and the people woke up to the silence of no call to prayer after five hundred years of hearing it five times every single day … just like how I was so used to hearing Mama's voice, her laughing, singing, and talking, and then one day I woke up and her voice wasn't there anymore … it was gone. But even though the people couldn't hear the call to prayer, they had it ringing in their hearts, so they actually could always hear it! Kinda like when I'm passing Mama's bedroom I can sometimes hear her laugh, or when I'm outside in our yard I can hear her talking to us from the porch! Subhanallah, Buraq! It's like she said it would be … as long as I love her, I can always hear her in my heart. Amazing.

Baba and Uncle Hasan took us to Fatih Mosque for the Friday prayer. On the way I told Baba what I had been told about the Sofia mosques. He told me that Grandma's uncle lived during the years in Turkey when the *adhan* became illegal in Arabic and had to be called in Turkish instead. Can you believe it, Buraq? Grandma's uncle couldn't bring himself to call it in Turkish so he called it in Arabic, and he was beaten to within an inch of his life and then sent to prison. He died there a few months later. I can't imagine what it would have been like to hear it called in Turkish.

Know what, Buraq? Now I know where my strong-willed spirit comes from! My great-great-uncle refused to do something he didn't believe in, and he comes from where I come from! I like to think I would have done the same thing he did.

We got to the mosque just in time, but we had to pray outside in the courtyard because the whole place was packed. I have never seen so many people in one place praying together. And the sermon by the imam was strange. I can understand Auntie Ayshe and Grandma, and I spoke Turkish with Mama, but I could hardly understand anything he was saying. On the way home Uncle Hasan was talking to Baba about it in English; it was about how, when we are grateful for things, Allah gives us more. A while ago I worried that Mama died because I was not grateful enough for her, but when I told Mrs. Prouty this, she reassured me that it couldn't be true. After I had been with Grandma for a little while, I started to really feel Mama between us, just from a different place.

I have to go—Auntie Ayshe is calling me for dinner.

Saturday, June 12 | 10

I slept for eighteen hours! I missed the night prayer and the morning prayer. I can't believe I slept through the *adhans* for two prayers. Baba said he tried to wake me both times but he couldn't even get me to moan! But I feel so much better now.

You know what I realized, Buraq? When we were sitting in the car at the airport I was feeling so much pain I thought my heart would burst. But do you know what? It was different to the pain I felt when Mama first died. I mean, when she died it seemed my whole world was caving in and I didn't know how I would be able to keep living without her. But I have kept living ... there have been some really hard times, but I haven't broken like I thought I would. I have even been happy sometimes. It seems like life has gotten bigger, like more things are possible—it's like the pain is a smaller thing inside a much larger me. The fear part of it isn't there anymore, but the love part of it is, and especially the peace part of it that Baba taught me at the waterfall.

Grandma has cats everywhere. She buys sheep lungs and cooks them with bread every three days and the cats have a feast. Lots of people all over the city feed the cats this way, that's why I call Istanbul the "City of Cats". They are so fun to watch, how they tumble through the lavender at the front of the house, which by the way has overtaken the garden and is about to eat the house. Then they leap onto the walls and then from there to the roof where they sit and clean each other with their raspy tongues. Wherever you go in the city you will find little old ladies feeding them, and most don't buy cat food, they cook up things in their own kitchens. Sheep lungs are cheap and cats love them!

Sunday, June 13 | 10

Grandma and I have been out in her yard all day today. She is puttering around with her lavender. I helped her pull out some of the old woody bushes to make room for new growth. She started remembering what it was like when Mama was a little girl. She told me the most amazing thing today: Mama was born and died on the same day, according to the Islamic calendar! The third of Rajab, one of the sacred months! Grandma went on to tell me the story of the day Mama was born. They were near Konya at Lake Beysehir while Grandpa was studying the birds and wildlife of the local wetlands. I always knew he studied wildlife but I didn't know any details. It's funny, I remember Mama telling me how the water levels were falling there and many of the marshlands had all but dried up. Grandma says that Grandpa saw these problems coming because of the way they were irrigating the farmland, but nobody would listen. Anyway, Grandma said she had gone out with him on a watch and she felt her baby kicking really hard, so hard she almost fell out of the boat! Grandpa (my hero) rushed her back to the village and they called the midwife. She said Mama was born just a few hours later, just after the most amazing sunset over the lake. She remembers it was the third of Rajab because that is one of the sacred months leading up to Ramadan, and her favorite month.

Tuesday, June 15 | 10

We went to the Panorama 1453 Museum today. I have never seen anything like it. Yasemin's dad has told me lots of stories about the conquest of Istanbul in 1453, but it was really amazing to see what they have done with the Panorama. It is inside a giant dome. The walls holding up the dome are painted from floor to ceiling—or I should say from floor to dome—with the most beautiful depictions of the sky, and the old Byzantine walls, the cavalry, soldiers, pack animals, trees, meadows, and all kinds of other scenery.

The floor has real figures and all kinds of museum artifacts that complete the scenes painted on the walls and dome. In the very center is a big platform visitors can stand on. And you can even listen from a set of headphones to stories about what is happening in the paintings and exhibits in each direction. Mehmed was delighted. He and Baba stayed all day. Auntie Ayshe and I left at lunchtime. I think Mehmed will be a scholar of Ottoman history! When he came home he sat with Grandma and told her stories about what he saw there. He remembered things I hadn't even seen, that's for sure! Grandma was delighted, and very impressed. She is such a good listener.

Wednesday, June 16 | 10

This morning right after *fajr* Grandma and Mehmed and I
went to the neighborhood weekly market and found sour
cherries! They are called *vishne* here. Grandma bought
five kilos. We had to clean them and pit them and then we
layered them with sugar in great big bowls and put them
in the refrigerator. Tomorrow, when the juice has been
released, we'll drain it off, bottle it, and add more sugar to
the cherries. We'll keep doing this until the cherries refuse
to give us any more juice, and then we'll bottle them too,
to use for decorating cakes! In the winter it will be easy to
make glasses of juice with this concentrate. Wish I would
be here then! Wish I could take some home to Canada!
Wish we had sour cherries in Canada. The other normal
cherries, the ones we have in Canada (they call them *kiraz*
here), just won't do the same thing, and they don't have that
wild, mysterious flavor the sour cherries have. The other
reason I love them is that Baba says they are his favorite
fruit in all the world.

Thursday, June 17 | 10

Today Grandma and I made *dolma*, stuffed grape leaves. We fried lots of onions and pine nuts in olive oil on her little old stove and then added rice, currants ("bird raisins" in Turkish!), parsley, dill, salt, pepper, sugar ... Yum. Oh, and I forgot to say ... they have cinnamon and mint too. Then we took the pots and boards and flash-boiled leaves out into the garden by the lilac bushes and rolled them on the big garden table. I remember before Mama got sick she used to make them sometimes, and I would help her roll them. Oh, she was so patient with me. Mama, can't you come back, and see how tight I can roll them now?

In the afternoon we all took a ferry trip out to Emirgan and ate in a fish restaurant.

Friday, June 18 | 10

Today we went to Eyup Sultan Mosque for the Friday prayer. I wrote a letter to Yasemin to share with Janine and Hana. Here's a little of it.

Greetings, my dear friends, from the great city of Istanbul! I am writing to tell you about my most favorite mosque in the whole world ... or should I say mosque complex, for it has a few different parts, the best of which is the huge hillside-cemetery that runs up onto a ridge overlooking the Golden Horn. Here you can sit and drink tea and watch the sights at Pierre Loti Cafe... Now, dear friends, you probably think I'm creepy to be going on like this about a cemetery, but just give me a chance to try and describe the beauty of this place. It is packed with the most amazing gravestones, carved into shapes like turbans, or books, or incredible lacy designs! And the Ottoman script, like Arabic, dances across them, carved in the stone. There's a little stone path leading up and up, and often it turns into a stairway. And there are green plants growing everywhere ... across the path, up the stairs, between the gravestones. The graves are all piled on top of each other. Oh, I wish we could bring Mama and bury her here, because she was like these people, and then she could be here among people like herself. She made Allah the title of her life. I know she really missed the sound of the call to prayer when she was in Canada ... here she could hear it all the time.

Saturday, June 19 | 10

Oh, Buraq, I can't sleep! What a good friend you are, always ready for me! Everyone's asleep in Grandma's tiny house so I'm hiding under my blanket with a flashlight! I can't stop thinking about Mama, Buraq, after visiting the graveyard. I walked up all the steps of the cemetery to the very top yesterday, past the higgledy-piggledy graves, and then just ahead the horizon stretches out forever. When I looked at it I realized it didn't matter, all the crowding and the bustling and the changes and all the things we keep ourselves busy with and all the things we are afraid of, because the beauty will always bring us back to the horizon stretching into forever ... Mama's beauty is here with me, even though her cocoon-shard lies all the way across on the other side of the world in a little piece of ground.

Shhh! I think I hear somebody waking up! Goodnight, Buraq!

Wednesday, June 23 | 10

Buraq, I was rereading our lovely conversations in this book—it is almost getting full, you know—and I noticed some things about Baba. He was such a brave man ... he never felt he had to hide from anyone because of his tears, he just kept waiting until his voice would work again, he didn't back down from what was happening. I saw for the first time that when Mama died, he was losing his best friend, it wasn't just me who was losing my mother. I really pray that I will be able to help him and take care of him always. I will never forget how good he has been to me.

Today we are going home to Toronto. Buraq, I have been crying all day. If I had known how hard it would be to tear myself away from Grandma and Auntie Ayshe, I might not have been willing to come in the first place. How have I lived without them all these years? How will I manage back in Toronto? I feel worse than when Mama first died.

Thursday, July 1 | 10

Good old Uncle Furqan picked us up from the airport. He was grinning from ear to ear and told us he had a surprise for us. When we got home we could smell fried chicken and chocolate cake before we even got inside. Mrs. Prouty!!! She came back a week ago, and Uncle Furqan decided to keep it a secret and surprise us, instead of telling us on Skype, like he told us all the other news.

You know, Buraq, I was apprehensive as we were driving home—the home where Mama no longer is—but it was like she was there with us, and had been with us all the way home, and we were coming home together.

Saturday, July 3 | 10

Uncle Furqan stayed over so we've had lots of time to tell him all about our trip. We brought him some hand-made shoes from Safranbolu, some freeze-dried white mulberries, and a new leather briefcase. This morning, after he made us pancakes (yummm!), we went hiking and found two new chrysalises and five caterpillars. So we're setting up the tank again. It feels like it's been a long time.

Sunday, July 4 | 10

Next week we are going to do a gathering for the second anniversary of Mama's death. Mrs. Prouty was asking me what we should serve. Mama used to love fresh pineapple ... so I suggested a big fruit salad with strawberries and mangoes and fresh pineapple. And pineapple and coconut milk smoothies.

Saturday, July 10 | 10

Today was the gathering. So many people came, Buraq.
Yasemin and Hana stayed over last night with me. We
stayed up half the night talking and laughing. They are such
good friends. They wanted to hear all about Turkey and
especially about Grandma. Today Grandma and Auntie
Ayshe called on Skype too. How I wish they could have
been here! Yasemin and Hana listened in and said they
loved hearing our Turkish! Chloe, Janine, and Amy are all
away for the summer.

The ladies started coming after the noon prayer. Three
nurses came from the hospital. They brought Mrs.
Hildebrand again, the head nurse from the sick kids'
hospital. I never wrote about her, Buraq. She came last
year for the first-year anniversary and she asked me if I
would be willing to go in and visit some of the kids on the
oncology unit there. Buraq, I just flat out refused. There was
no way I wanted to go anywhere near them. I didn't want
to be reminded of Mama at all, no way. Well, she wanted to
hear all about how I was doing and what I was doing. She
saw Mehmed's chrysalis tank and wanted to hear about it.

When I told her, she asked me again to consider coming to the outpatient unit and sharing it with the kids there. Well, Buraq, you know, I think I'd like to do it after all.

Monday, July 12 | 10

Buraq, today I went to the hospital for the first day of my volunteer work. Mrs. Hildebrand took me on a tour where I met some of the kids. I saw one little girl aged about four. Her name is Sally. She was so sweet! She had lost all her hair and she was playing with a doll that had no hair either! One of the girls is Muslim. She's from Lebanon. She's around 13, I think, and her name is Taqwa. Her own language is Arabic but she knows English really well. There were three other girls, Mary, who is 10, and Janet and Cynthia who are both 11, and two boys: Carl is 12 and Sam is 9.

Buraq, it is so sad. Mrs. Hildebrand said later that Taqwa is one of the children they are most concerned about. This is her third trip to the unit. They brought her all the way from Lebanon the first time when she was only eight. At first her treatments were working well and then all of a sudden they stopped working, and now her doctors feel they can do nothing more for her. She's getting sicker and sicker really fast. I can't stop thinking about her.

Tuesday, July 13 | 10

Baba has printed out our photos from Turkey so I am putting them in an album today. I just still can't get used to seeing family photos without Mama.

Wednesday, July 14 | 10

At the oncology unit today little Sally was telling me she'll
be going home soon. I thought she meant going home, you
know, going back to her house, but she looked up at me
and said, "Daddy says the angels will take me and it won't
hurt at all." Subhanallah, Buraq, I almost fell on the floor.
I don't know where my actions came from or where the
words came from but they rolled off my tongue and only
afterwards did I realize it was a prayer. I picked her up—she
was as light as a feather—and I said, "May Allah make it easy
for you!" She pulled my face close to hers and kissed me.

Mrs. Hildebrand came up to me and told me I was just like
Mama!

Thursday, July 15 | 10

Buraq, you know, I love being at the hospital. Today was my second day with Suzanne, my "big sister" for volunteering. I basically just followed her around the unit and listened and watched. She's really funny and the kids just love her. All except Taqwa, who won't talk to her. Suzanne says she remembers Taqwa from her last visit and can't believe how she has changed. She said her parents last brought her about two years ago, when she was 11. She was really sweet and generous then, and they are surprised by how much she has changed. She hardly talks to anyone, she hardly even looks at anyone. Oh Buraq, it made me so sad. Her mother just sits there near her bed looking unhappy. When I said "salams" to her, she nearly jumped out of her chair to greet me. Taqwa, on the other hand, just sneered at me ... she wouldn't answer my greeting, and she just turned away, in her tight pants and her shirt that slides up over her belly, and her frizzy bushy hair.

Friday, July 16 | 10

Today, Uncle Furqan is taking us on a trip. We'll drive east from here along the northern shore of Lake Ontario to Long Point. We are going for the whole weekend.

Saturday, July 17 | 10

Sleeping down next to the lake—it is so quiet. Mehmed is already sleeping and there are so many stars that I can just barely see the page to write this. More in the morning! G'night!

Sunday, July 18 | 10

The sun is rising over the lake, Buraq, and the sky is shot with rose and dark streaks of lavender and the palest of greens ... come to think of it, almost chrysalis green. The water is perfectly still. I prayed *fajr* on the dock because the grass was so wet. Last night as I was falling asleep under the stars I started to remember something that happened soon after Mama died, something I had never even written to you about. Buraq, one night alone in my room the pain got so bad, I was feeling so angry, that I just wrapped up my Qur'an and put it on a shelf in my closet. And I took up all my hijabs and stuffed them in a bag on the floor of my closet. Something in me just shut down and I intended to go to school with my hair flowing everywhere for everyone to see and I never intended to open my Qur'an again. As long as Mama was gone, what did it matter anymore? I might as well just do whatever I wanted; it all seemed broken. I didn't even pray the night prayer. I remember feeling how rigid my heart felt, and I kept saying, I'm just not gonna do this anymore, if it's going to be like this. I felt Allah had hurt me and I wanted to turn my back on Him.

That night I dreamed of Mama. She was on the other side of a chasm that cut right down into the earth so deep I couldn't see the bottom. She was wearing a long white gown and she had white and pink roses entwined through her hair. She was standing on a thick green carpet of grass. The moment I saw her, I remembered I had put my Qur'an and scarves away, and I wanted to duck down and hide from her. But I heard her reciting the last verse of the Chapter *Al Baqara*, in the same voice she used to teach the verses to me so long ago—lilting, like water in a fountain, like doves in the evening. And those sounds entered my heart, and dissolved everything, and lifted me and carried me right across that chasm to her arms.

Allah does not tax any soul
but what it can bear:
it shall have all it earns,
and pay for but what it commits.
'O Lord, take us not to task if we forget or make a mistake;
O Lord, nor place upon us an unsuperable load
as You did on those just before us;
Nor then requite us with what we have no strength to withstand;
But pardon us, forgive us,
and show us bounteous mercy,

You are our Master: so give us triumph
over the people of the unbelievers.[1]

– Al Baqarah 2:286 –

Ohhh, her arms were so sweet, she was so sweet. I woke up then, but that sweetness was there in the room with me. I remember it was only about 3:30 in the morning. I went to the bathroom and saw that Baba was up praying, but I felt I had seen a great secret so I just washed for prayer and went right back to my room. All I could think about was covering my hair, Buraq, so I dug my scarves out of the closet. And then I did the night prayer. I dug out my Qur'an, my true friend, and read it until I heard Baba leave for the masjid. I fell asleep again after I prayed *fajr*. I still felt the sweetness in the morning, but it was different then, it just made me miss her all the more. By the following evening the feeling was gone. The whole thing just seemed like a distant dream, and I forgot all about it until last night. Subhanallah.

I see now that was the night I started to realize something. I had felt that Mama's death was breaking my life, and so I started to fight and scramble to do whatever I could to save myself and change things. Of course I knew I couldn't change anything, but it's as if my body, my mind, my heart,

didn't know that. Buraq, it was so strange ... that night, I felt myself soften, and sink down into the realm of "what is." I felt myself saying, OK, Allah, have it Your way ... I'm here ... I can cope ... Yes.

The next day everything seemed the same as before, and I forgot all about that acceptance. But now I see it never really vanished. In fact, that was the moment that the 'yes' started to grow. Now I see it is bigger in me, and I am more confident in it. Alhamdulillah.

Monday, July 19 | 10

Buraq, remember how I told you about how things are getting better for Mehmed since Baba started working from home? Today he offered to wash the dishes after lunch so I could get ready to go to the hospital. Can you believe it? I remember all the times Baba would do that for Mama if she was in a hurry.

Today we had a meeting with Mrs. Hildebrand. Do you know what she asked me, Buraq? She asked me if I would show my journal to them. I said I really didn't think I could do that, because it was just too personal. So she asked me if I could at least explain to Suzanne about the butterflies. Well, that's a lot easier! I told them all about the monarch's life cycle, and how the chrysalis is formed, and how the butterfly comes out. You know, Buraq, while I was telling them, I thought about Taqwa. Do you think she is stuck somewhere? She's like I was when I couldn't stand the thought of the beautiful green chrysalis turning black. I thought the chrysalis was an exquisite jewel. I wanted to own it, to make it mine, but it had to move on, it had to turn black or there would never have been a butterfly, the butterfly I love so much. There was no stopping it, and if I had been able to stop it, it would've been a great loss. I told this to Suzanne, and I just wanted to run to Taqwa, but Suzanne said no, she told me to wait, that she didn't think Taqwa would be willing to hear that from me.

Mrs. Hildebrand asked if I could set up a tank there at the hospital! What a wonderful idea! Maybe if Taqwa could see the chrysalis, and the butterfly that comes from it...

Tuesday, August 10 | 10

Tomorrow Ramadan begins. Mrs. Prouty came today and she made me bake *acma* and *simit* ... she just helped me here and there. Even Mehmed came in and twisted some dough and dipped the *simit* into the sesame seeds. But, ugh, what a mess he made!

Tonight we will do the Ramadan night prayers at the big mosque downtown. I have missed those prayers!

Wednesday, August 11 | 10

There is something about the end of the night, the time when it meets the morning, where everything seems uncovered and unprotected. When I got up for our Ramadan meal before sunrise, I was really surprised not to find Mama in the kitchen, and it was almost as painful as it used to be right after she died. But, alhamdulillah, it was a passing pain this time, because now there are so many other memories that ease the pain.

Today at the hospital Mrs. Hildebrand said she had got permission for the tank, so now I have to go chrysalis-hunting! It's been a long time!

Mary went home today. Too bad I never really got a chance to talk much to her.

Thursday, August 12 | 10

Oh, Buraq, I think maybe today was the hardest day I have spent at the hospital. First when I got there Suzanne told me that Sally died in the night. I was just shocked. I felt myself crumble into a chair. Suzanne said Sally's mother and father and grandmother were all here with her, but her mother had her heart set on taking her little girl home one last time. I felt so sad for her.

Taqwa was in a terrible mood. When I walked in she scowled at me. Her frizzy hair ringed her face and made her look fierce. I looked at her and for a split second I felt like I was looking at the little girl she was when she first came to this hospital. Suzanne had told me she was the cutest little girl then, who would spend her time memorizing the Qur'an. She was always listening to it on a little cassette recorder with headphones. She had her own little prayer rug and used it for all her prayers. She had a sweetness about her and everybody loved her to bits for it. And then she said, "So why are you wearing that stupid thing on your head?" I felt like she'd thrown a rock at me. I don't know where the words came from, but I told her it's because I love Allah and care about what He wants from me. She just rolled her eyes and made a big sarcastic face. She said, "Yeah, right, like He really cares anyway! What makes you think He even notices you?" Then she turned her face to the wall. I felt so sad ... I had no idea what to say then. I felt—again, for the second time that day—like all the wind had been knocked out of my sails. I was really glad that it was almost time to go home, because all I wanted was to be in my room with the blankets pulled up over my head. When I got home and walked past Mama's door, for a second it was as if I could hear her in there repeating Allah's name. I felt like I was going to explode. I threw myself on my bed and covered my head with a pillow, but I couldn't stay there. I leapt up again. The pit of my stomach was roaring, Buraq. I wanted to scream out to Allah, *She worked so hard for You! Why couldn't You have saved her? Why couldn't she be here now, where I need her?* And I kept hearing Taqwa's question: "*What makes you think He even notices you?*" I wanted so much to help her, and all I got was derision. How could I help her if I haven't been helped? I pounded my pillow on the bed until one of the seams split and feathers flew all over my room. O, Buraq, I wanted to just disappear. I sank down onto the floor next to my bed and lay there, unable to move.

I don't know how long I lay there, but after a while I opened my eyes and shifted my legs under me. When I did that, a few of the pillow feathers flew up into the air and as I followed one of them floating there, it occurred to me that if the 'yes' was gone, then in its place must be a 'no' ... a 'no?' I had this almost comical image of myself turning my head to look behind me as if to say, Who? Me? That really startled me, Buraq! Was I saying no somehow? How? To whom was I saying no?

And then it hit me. Had I not just said to Allah, "she worked so hard for You, why couldn't You have saved her?"

Well, who did I think I was, anyway? Who was I to evaluate what "working hard" is? Who am I to decide what "saving" might be?

Yikes! I have to pick up Mehmed from his soccer practice.

Thursday, August 12 | 10 *late evening*

Buraq, I soared across that field to the park! Like one of those feathers, soaring on an invisible current. We really don't know what is going on here! We think we do, but we do not. I kept remembering what Muhammad told us, may Allah bless him and give him peace.

> *"Remember Allah and He will remember you.*
> *Remember Allah and you will find Him on your side.*
> *If you lean on anything, lean on Allah. And know*
> *that if all the world came together to benefit you in something,*
> *they can only benefit you in something Allah has ordained for you.*
> *And if all the world came together to harm you in some way,*
> *they can only harm you in a way Allah has written for you*
> *The pen has been raised and the pages have dried."*

I suddenly remembered that there was still a possibility of finding chrysalises, and two minutes later I saw one on a low branch right near the path. Perfect! One for Taqwa! I found an old paper cup someone had tossed, so I broke off the branch the chrysalis was on and carried it with me.

Mehmed was in a bad mood because he felt he hadn't played well at soccer, and wasn't particularly interested for once.

Friday, August 13 | 10

You know, Buraq, I still cannot fathom all that happened
with me yesterday. I really miss Mama, and sometimes I still
feel mad that she's not here anymore. But something else
has come in now, since my "experience" yesterday ... I'm not
sure how I will be able to write it down ... I mean, I'm OK,
you know, Buraq? Not having my mother here is actually
nowhere as horrible as I imagined it would be. The first time
I heard she might die, way back when she first got sick,
it seemed a catastrophe ... but then life carried me along,
and each part was easier to actually live than I thought it
would be. When I look back I guess what I feel is that really
and truly Allah was there walking me through it all. Even
when I totally turned my back on Him, and really got mad
at Him, He never turned His back on me. I see now I was
like a little baby having a tantrum, and just like Baba never
used to hold Mehmed's tantrums against him, he would just
wait it out with him and then draw him closer when it was
finished, it's like Allah just waited out my tantrums and then
drew me closer, and by that time I was bigger somehow,
so I could embrace what *He* wanted to happen instead
of what *I* thought *must* happen. Honestly, Buraq, how can

I ever shrink from such a question as Taqwa asked me yesterday: "What makes you think He even notices you?" I *know* He notices me! I feel it as strongly as I feel my father noticing me!

Baba says maybe I have something to teach Taqwa. At first I asked what? I feel really afraid around her. How must it feel to know you might die? Even though Baba's been telling me since I was small that one day we will all die, and even though my own mother has died, still ... my own death? Taqwa's death? These are harder to think about. But, you know, the more I think about it, the more I just want to say to her, "You think Allah gave you the name Taqwa for *nothing*?"

Saturday, August 14 | 10

It took all morning for me and Mehmed and Uncle Furqan to find four more chrysalises in the big milkweed field down the road. (Mehmed had recovered from his soccer pout.) It's getting late in the season, or maybe this isn't a good year. I was getting so worried ... the opportunity to take chrysalises onto the unit at the hospital, for all the kids but for Taqwa especially, is too good to miss. Anyway, five will be enough, inshallah. Then Baba took me to buy a fish tank, and he made a screen top for it. Mehmed brought me a beautiful gnarled branch of maple to prop up inside in the corner.

Tonight we went to Baba's friends and broke our fast with them. After *iftar* we did the *taraweeh* prayer in the downtown mosque. Uncle Furqan came back home with us to make us pancakes for *sahur*!

Monday, August 16 | 10

Baba helped me take the tank to the hospital. Carl and Sam were the most interested in it. Carl is in the worst days of chemo, and still he wanted to hear every detail about where and how we found the cocoons, and what would happen to them. Sam said he'd seen them on television. Taqwa was the only one who didn't make any effort to see it. When people are around she mostly just lies in bed looking at the wall. I worked up my courage and went over to say "salams" ... she just murmured an answer but kept staring at the wall. I didn't know what to say. Of course I knew what I wanted to say. I wanted to blurt out all the ways Allah had helped me understand last Thursday, the day Sally died, the day Taqwa threw her 'rock' at me, you know, the day I caught myself saying 'no' to Allah ... but obviously I knew that would never work, at least not now.

Tuesday, August 17 | 10

Today when I got to the hospital Suzanne was having a conversation with Taqwa's mother. Suzanne had given Taqwa some paper and pastels and invited her to draw. Taqwa just threw the pastels on the floor. Her mother told Suzanne that the doctor had been there yesterday evening and explained to Taqwa that the new lab results showed them that the experimental treatment would not work. Her poor mom told Taqwa that her dad was coming over from Lebanon in two weeks to take them back home. As soon as Taqwa heard that she said, "No! I don't want to go home! I want to stay here and get better!" After that she hadn't spoken and when Suzanne approached her she threw the pastels.

I just wanted to hold her, but she wouldn't let me near her. I asked if she'd seen the chrysalises. "I couldn't care less," was what she said. I started to walk away. I felt stung, and wished I hadn't said anything, and then I remembered the tantrum factor. All of a sudden Mama's reassuring words bubbled up out of my heart. I turned back and stood as close to her as I could get. "Taqwa," I said. "Wait. You wil see. I promise, Allah is cherishing you, you just don't see it yet."

She looked at me and started to say something, and then it was as if her words just evaporated in her mouth.

Wednesday, August 18 | 10

Buraq, poor Taqwa is so angry and today I realized something. She doesn't have anybody to tell about it. I was thinking about this last night, and I remembered what Mrs. Prouty was saying to me—the difference for me would be that I have a lot of people who love me, and to me that means a lot of people who can hear about my worst faults and not judge me. Like Baba. Like you, Buraq! When I have said or written awful things, other people's love has always helped me find my way back again. Well, who's listening to Taqwa? Her mother, poor thing, seems too scared herself. Maybe Suzanne could listen to her, but Suzanne hasn't lost anybody close to her.

Thursday, August 19 | 10

Oh Buraq, where to begin?

This morning at *fajr* I asked Allah to show me how to help Taqwa. I went back to sleep and when I woke up again I went straight to Mama's closet and pulled out her quilt! She loved it so much and said it helped her ... would it help Taqwa? I couldn't wait to get to the hospital and give it to her. I wasn't worried at all about how mean she might be to me.

I decided not to even say anything to her, just to lay it out on her bed. For once I actually remembered to tell Allah I was intending my action for His sake alone.

When I got there, she wasn't on the unit, and neither was her mother. They had taken her downstairs for a test, so while they were gone I spread it out over her bed and then just went to check in with the other kids. First I got Sam and we went to check on the chrysalis tank. Nothing new. The chrysalises were in the same places we had put them in before, one hanging from its stick that we had lashed to the screen with thread, two on milkweed branches leaning up against Mehmed's gnarled maple, and one hanging from a stick propped in the corner. Sam told me again all about what he had seen on television and I have to say I was glad he never mentioned the part about the butterfly coming out first with a huge fat body and tiny little wings, so now he'll have a surprise seeing it in real life.

Still Taqwa wasn't back on the ward.

I went to see Carl, poor thing. He was still feeling rotten from his treatment. His mother was there with his little sister Patty. Then I saw Taqwa and her mother pass the door on the way to their room, I didn't want to seem like I was running after them so I stayed where I was, holding Patty on my lap.

About five minutes later Suzanne came to get me. She pulled me out in the hall and told me that when Taqwa went into her room, she stopped and ran her hand along the quilt. When she found out that I had put it there, she immediately got in bed and curled up under it. I guess she likes it!

Friday, August 20 | 10

I've been trying to read a part of the Qur'an a day for Ramadan but I'm already behind. Baba suggested that I read with the recordings as it would go faster, so this afternoon I'm locking myself in my room. I keep remembering how the Angel Jibril would come to Muhammad, may Allah bless him and give him peace, and go through the whole Qur'an with him every year during Ramadan. Since Allah has given me the ability to go through it too, how can I turn Him down? When I was with Grandma in Istanbul she told me she started reading the whole Qur'an in Ramadan when she was only eight!

Saturday, August 21 | 10

Alhamdulillah! I'm caught up with my Qur'an now.

Baba is taking us to the waterfall for a picnic *iftar*! We haven't had a good outing since the trip Uncle Furqan took us on after we got back from Istanbul. We have meatballs and spinach pies that Baba got from the Ramadan Bazaar at the mosque, and I am starving! I got up a little late this morning and didn't have time to eat as much as I wanted.

Monday, August 23 | 10

Well, Buraq, things were sure different at the hospital with Taqwa today.

I went into her room. Her mother wasn't there so I just sat down next to the bed. At first she just turned her face away like usual. I told her she looked pretty under the colors of the quilt, almost as pretty as my mother had.

"Your mother?" she said.

"This quilt was a gift I gave to my mother when she was sick. She loved geometric designs and bright colors, especially these colors on the quilt." I told her all about the day I was trying to do my homework and then had the idea to buy the quilt. All the time I was talking to her, Buraq, I thought that she understood my intention, which was just to share a story with her. But no. She got more and more agitated. I just missed all her cues.

"Well, why did you take it away from her? Why'd you give it to me?"

Then I suddenly realized I had made a big mistake. But there was no turning back. When I said the words "she died" to her, something broke in me. Do you know, Buraq, in all these two years, I haven't had to say those words to anyone. Everyone always knew the truth already. My eyes were hot and then wet and my lips were starting to fly out of control.

Taqwa took one look at me, jumped out of bed, and ran to the window. I felt scared and I knew she did too. I felt really surprised by how hot my tears were and, before I knew it, my whole face was awash. I felt so stupid. I'm supposed to be here to help her, and look at me.

She sat down beside the window, put her head on the windowsill and remained still. I started to pray for help ... I should say my tongue started to pray for help, because it just happened spontaneously. And then I remembered Mama saying, *Wait*. The words just drifted up so easily in me, like the lightest whisper-wisp of a cloud in a blue sky. *You will see. Allah is cherishing you.* And in that moment I *knew* that Allah *is* cherishing me. It was as if the whole world stopped turning for a moment, and everything that was happening seemed totally right. I took a big breath. It felt as if someone was saying, OK, this is the way Allah wrote this moment, let's see what the next one brings. I remembered that I didn't need to be afraid of Taqwa, that she is hurting and scared. So I went to her, stood where she would see me, and smiled at her. I told her it's been two years since Mama died and that I have never had to tell anyone, because I've always only been around family and close friends who already knew. So when my voice and tongue said it, it was like hearing it for the first time, and feeling it for the first time. I asked her to please ask Allah to bless Mama in her grave.

Right away she said, "*Inna lillahi wa inna ilayhi raji'un*" —surely we belong to God and to Him shall we return. But then she lifted her head and looked at me. She asked me how, if my mother died, I could just stand there like that.

I sat down on the lavender-colored bedspread. I was starting to feel a little relieved. "Well, Taqwa," I said, "in two years I've done a lot of crying, believe me. I've had some really hard times, and even some times when I wanted to turn my back on Allah because I felt He'd hurt me."

Her eyes widened. Funny, I'd never seen them change like that.

"You did? You wanted to turn your back on Him?"

"Yes. One night I even packed away my Qur'an and all my scarves."

"Really? What happened then?"

I told her about seeing Mama in my dream, and hearing her voice recite the last verse of the Chapter *Al Baqara*.

Buraq, the moment I said "Baqara," Taqwa leaned against the back of the chair and recited the last verses of that chapter: "La yukalifu lahu nafsan illah wus'a'ha"—on no soul does Allah place a burden greater than it can bear. Her voice was so beautiful. She stopped all of a sudden, as if she thought she'd made a mistake. I told her I loved her recitation, but when I asked her to continue she just shook her head. I went back to what I had been saying. I told her that when I heard Mama's voice in my dream I became the tiny little girl memorizing that verse at her knees ... when I woke up I felt her sweetness and all I wanted was to pray, so obviously I had to dig through my closet and find that sack of hijabs!

She sat forward again and just looked at the floor. She said she'd never wanted to pray. It was always something she had to do, and she stopped praying a long time ago and never saw a dream making her want to go back to it. "I could never be like you," she said.

"Well, Taqwa," I said, " maybe Allah is giving you something bigger than a dream to bring you back, ever think about that?"

"What do you mean?"

"Sometimes the most beautiful things are made by difficulty. Take the butterfly, for instance. When I first saw a chrysalis I thought it was the most beautiful thing I'd ever seen. When I found out it had to turn black and fall away, I was so upset ... until I saw the incredible butterfly coming out of it. Or what about a simple apple? First there is this beautiful, pink-tinged apple blossom, and only when that dies and falls apart does the apple start to grow. Part of the process is the falling apart of the beautiful flower ... if you just wanted the flower to stay the way it is, you'd never get to the apple."

Then she just kinda snapped. "You're just crazy, talking to me about butterflies and diamonds and apples! And what was that you said to me the other day? Allah is cherishing me? How can you say He is cherishing me? He made me sick in the first place. I thought He was caring for me when the treatments started to work, but then they stopped working and I started getting sicker and sicker. So how am I supposed to believe He is cherishing me? Or do you call this cherishing?" She flicked her hand across her bony bare belly between her shirt and her jeans.

She flung herself up out of the chair and went back to her bed. She gathered up the quilt in her hands and dumped it into the chair. "And take this dead woman's quilt, I don't need it."

Ouch, Buraq! I wanted to scream ... but somehow Allah made me remember the tantrum factor. I just said, in as light and friendly a voice as I could muster, "We can talk later, habibti. Get some rest," and walked out, leaving the quilt where it was.

But I felt really shaken.

I went to see Mrs. Hildebrand and told her about everything. I was surprised—she was really positive about it. She says Taqwa is angry at God and feels her life is being snatched away from her. She feels ripped off that all the wretched treatments have gotten her nowhere. She says until Taqwa can work through this, she and everyone around her will be miserable. She thinks it was a good thing that Taqwa did something as outrageous as rolling up and tossing the quilt, because she had already told Suzanne how much she loved it. "Don't worry, my dear," she said to me. "Give her a few days to think about all the incredible things you've shown her and said to her. It was a really good opening, her saying all those things. You know, your mother would be so proud of you."

Mama would be proud of me? Maybe so, but ... how I wish I could tell her about Taqwa!

Tuesday, August 24 | 10

Carl and Sam came running to me today to show me that one of the chrysalises had gone dark. Alhamdulillah, they were so excited. It was hard to convince them to keep their hands off it, though! Taqwa's mother even came to look. I drew some sketches to show her what would happen.

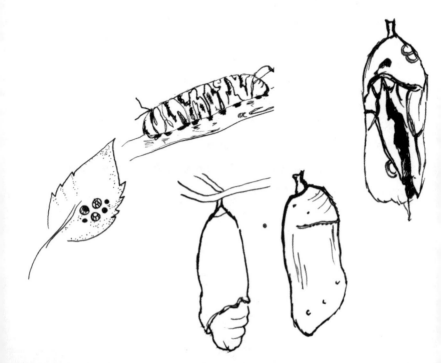

Wednesday, August 25 | 10

Well, Buraq, I am really surprised, but Mrs. Hildebrand was right. Today I went to the unit and there was Taqwa, curled up in Mama's quilt (can you believe it?) by the fish tank, watching the chrysalis! Subhanallah! It was transparent this morning and you could see the wings folded up inside. When she saw me she said, "It really has gone all ugly! Is this how it's supposed to be?" Carl, bless his little heart, said, "Well of course, silly! The chrysalis has to fall away or else the butterfly will never fly!"

Well, the outer covering cracked and the butterfly's wing was sticking out. Now the covering was transparent. By this time Cynthia and Janet had come (with their blankets!) and a new girl, Patricia, who is nine. Everyone was glued to the spot. Suzanne finally came too, and Mrs. Hildebrand. Even the nurses and orderlies stopped to look and sit whenever they could steal a few minutes from their chores. At one point even the chief administrator of the hospital came and sat with us on the floor! We were all there watching, Buraq! I wanted to jump up and dance, I was so happy. I never dreamed it would work out like this!

It took another half hour for the butterfly to get all the way free from its cocoon that now looked like a little plastic bag. It was still hanging from its perch propped against the maple branch, and the butterfly was hanging on to it for dear life. Pretty soon the butterfly fell down to the floor of the tank and just lay there.

The kids got really worried. "Is it dead? What's wrong with it, Nur?"

"Hey! This guy's not gonna fly anywhere! Look how small his wings are!"

"Don't worry," I told them. "Just keep watching!"

Soon enough, the butterfly got itself upright and started teetering around, dragging its enormous body behind it. But over the next hour as we sat and watched the butterfly's wings started to grow, and the body started to shrink. Before we knew it, it was stretching them all the way open, and folding them closed. The kids were convinced that it was getting ready to fly. The administrator called a janitor to open the window-screen, and we put the tank next to it so the butterfly could fly out whenever it wanted. And fly it did! And everybody cheered! Only Taqwa stayed quiet, hidden in her quilt on the floor.

Thursday, August 26 | 10

I wondered what kind of mood I would find Taqwa in when I went into the hospital today. I wanted to give her plenty of space, so first I visited all the other kids and went to her room last. As usual she was curled up in her bed. Alhamdulillah, she was under the quilt at least. She didn't lift her head, but she said, "Did you see? Another chrysalis is starting to darken." She was the first one to notice it. Secretly, I gave an unseen thumbs-up and a silent "YES!"

Friday, August 27 | 10 *morning*

Baba wants to have a big *iftar* at our house on Sunday night so today Mrs. Prouty and I are rolling *dolma*. We are using grape leaves she picked herself back in May and put in the freezer, and a yummy filling with brown rice, mint, dill, pine nuts, cinnamon, and little tiny bird raisins. Love it!

Saturday, August 28 | 10 ^{Morning}

I woke up with the most wonderful idea, Buraq, and Baba thought so too! We are going to invite Taqwa and her mother to the iftar! Uncle Furqan will go and bring them here. I am going to call Mrs. Hildebrand first, and then if she thinks it will work, she will call the hospital and arrange things. I am so excited! Mrs. Prouty and I are roasting big legs of lamb all shot through with garlic and tarragon, yummy!

Saturday, August 28 | 10 ^{afternoon}

Buraq! Subhanallah, you will never ever believe how Allah arranges things! Mrs. Hildebrand was really happy about our idea. She said that Taqwa has been stable, but she has just been staying in bed because she was depressed. She called the hospital and then called me back. Taqwa's doctors think it will be great for her to have a change of scene but the most amazing thing, Buraq, is that her father arrived last night from Lebanon and he is coming too! When Baba heard that he said, "Well, in that case let's invite them to stay the night! We can put her parents in the guest room and if Taqwa wants to, she can stay in yours; what do you think?" Then there was another flurry of telephone calls ... and we'll have a houseful of guests!

Sunday, August 29 | 10

She brought the quilt, Buraq. The quilt! She wanted to sleep in my room. Her doctors said she could go 24 hours with no IVs and they even took out her needle. Subhanallah, she looked so much better. Baba and Uncle Furqan had a great visit with her father. Baba's other friends really enjoyed meeting him too, because he is a journalism professor at the American University in Beirut. Baba said they talked for a long time after *iftar*. Mrs. Prouty stayed, and she and the other ladies, the wives of Baba's friends, were having a great time sharing recipes and talking about food. So Taqwa and I went to my room early. Mehmed stayed with the men.

After a little while I went downstairs to see if Mrs. Prouty needed any help. When I came back to my room, Taqwa was sitting on my settee. I took off my long coat and hung it on a hook behind the door. I tossed my lavender scarf on the back of the settee and ran my fingers through my hair.

"Your hair is so pretty," she said. "I'm happy to see it."

"Thanks, Taqwa. I'm so glad you are here in my room!"

She had a hundred questions. "Were you in this house

when your mother was sick? Did she do all the gardening? What did she do for work? What did your little brother do? How long ago did she get sick?" And then, "What did she do when the doctors said they couldn't help her anymore?"

"Taqwa," I told her. "I think of all the memories I have of her. What did she do? She just kept enjoying her life. She kept loving us. I didn't see her complain. I saw her cry some-times, and I saw her lose her temper, but only for a moment here and there. She was always the first to apologize and quick to forgive, and frequently asked us to pray for her." I suddenly felt a little scared, Buraq, and wondered if I was saying more than she wanted to hear. But she just settled herself a little deeper into the creamy settee and started fingering the dusty-rose throw. So I continued. "And the thing I found most amazing is that even after the treatments failed her, she kept on reading the Qur'an, saying extra prayers in the morning and at night. I remember wondering why she was doing all that, as it obviously wasn't work-ing. But now I know why—she just really, really loved Allah. She had always loved Him. He was her first concern and, mashallah, I can really see how easy He made things for her."

She sat up again. "But how can you say that, Nur? She didn't make it!"

"Taqwa, how can we know what 'making it' really is? Who

are we to tell Allah how long we should live? All I know was that even then it seemed she was blossoming into something bigger, and there was so much light. I am telling you that my experience with the chrysalis in those days stopped me short. The first time I saw one, I told you in the hospital, I fell in love with it ... its indescribable green color, it's amazing waxy surface, its magnificent gold necklace. Then we brought it home and one day it turned black. I was heartbroken!"

"Come on, Nur!" Taqwa replied.

"No, really, I was. I didn't want it to change."

"But if it didn't change, how could the butterfly get out? Would you rather choke the butterfly just to keep the cocoon?" Taqwa said.

"You see, Taqwa? You are wiser than I was. Without thinking, yes, I would almost have been willing to do that. But what a loss! That's when I started to see that what was happening to Mama was like what was happening to the chrysalis. She was about to change into something much greater. And it hit me even harder when I saw that butterfly fall out. You saw how it was that day we watched it in the hospital. The body was huge, and the wings were so small, and I thought, come on, how can he possibly fly like that? There must be something wrong. Remember how over the next hour the body shrank and the wings expanded? It reminded me exactly of what was happening to her … her body was shrinking so she could fly to Allah. It's much better to have the chrysalis for a short time, and to know it will eventually give way to something even more wonderful, the butterfly. Well, Allah has been telling us since the time of Adam that our lives are like that—they will eventually give way to something greater, and everything about Mama's death has shown me that is true. And the other thing I'll tell you is that none of this, none of it, was as horrible or as hard as I imagined it would be. That's not to say it wasn't hard, Taqwa, believe me. And it is still hard sometimes. Sometimes it was so hard I couldn't even see or feel the things I am telling you now. Or I was sure they were just fantasy. Sometimes I would just want to give up, or throw a tantrum, or break this house apart with my fists … but every time, something would happen and I would find my way again."

I stopped then because I could see her eyes filling up with tears. I just put my hand on hers, and didn't say anything, and then she broke down, and I just let her cry. Finally she picked up my little purple velvet pillow and hugged it.

"Nur, I am scared. I'm scared about what will happen to me," Taqwa said.

"Habibti, of course you are scared. Actually we should all

be scared, because we are so totally weak and helpless in the face of death. We all need to learn how to ask for help, to put ourselves in the hands of the One who created us in the first place. He loves being asked. And do you know, we actually have to ask for help for everything, not just the big things. Think about it. If the Prophet Muhammad prayed for help fixing his sandal, what are we doing? Subhanallah."

"I want my life, Nur. I want to grow up and work, and have a family. Why can't I just get better and grow up like everybody else? It makes me so mad!" She flung the pillow across the room onto the wicker rocking chair.

"I know, Taqwa. I wanted my mother to live. I wanted her— I still want her—to be here to help me grow up! I remember feeling so hurt to discover that all of our efforts weren't enough, and all of our prayers were not going to change what Allah had written. No amount of crying made any difference. We really are so helpless. And then in the end— we just have to finally realize it's not always about what we want. Life is so much bigger than we can imagine."

She curled up into a ball on the settee. I covered her with the throw. "I'm scared," she said. "I am scared about my mother. I'm so afraid of hurting her."

"You don't need to worry about your mother. Leave her to Allah. He has promised Paradise to any mother who bears the loss of her child with patience."

She lifted her head and looked at me. She looked so scared.

"But I have turned away from Allah. Will He forgive me?" she said.

"Forgive you? Mercy is Allah's first and foremost Name."

I sat down on the floor next to the settee. I could remember weeping on this same settee and Baba sitting here, reassuring me, just holding me inside his own peace until I could find my own.

I wanted to put some peace into her like it seemed Baba did for me that day.

"Taqwa," I said, "Allah Himself told us, 'My Mercy overspreads My Wrath,' and as a way of proving that to us, who are so weak in belief, He has made the very cells of our bodies as a mirror of that. Believe me, He is just waiting for us to ask, waiting for us to remember that we didn't create ourselves; waiting for us to remember that we aren't the ones keeping our hearts beating, our lungs inflating and deflating, our cells dividing. We need Him, and He is waiting for us, and for every step we take toward Him, He takes ten towards us."

She didn't say anything for a long time, and I didn't want to push anything so I just got up and went to check on the ladies. Taqwa's mother wanted to say goodnight to her so we came back up and found her in the same place on the settee, fast asleep. She had taken the lavender scarf I had left there and wrapped it around her head.

Her mother lowered herself to the floor beside the settee. "Ya Allah, she is so beautiful."

She put her head down beside her girl and started to weep.

Oh, Buraq, where is Mama?

Monday, August 30 | 10   *morning*

What a fun *sahur*! I don't think I've ever had a meal before the fast with guests who weren't family before! We had leftover *dolma* and Baba made a sweet bread for us before we woke up. The whole house smelled heavenly. Mehmed even got up on his own! You probably won't believe this, Buraq, but Taqwa wore the lavender scarf to breakfast, along with the purple and green robe I lent her. She looks so nice in it, I think I will just let her have it. You should have seen her dad's face when she came in ... but he was cool, he just greeted her with a huge smile.

Monday, August 30 | 10 *evening*

Buraq, it seems like two days have passed from *sahur* this morning until now. I am so tired, but I can't sleep until I write what happened today. It was one of the most amazing days of my life.

Baba had another crazy idea at *sahur*. "Let's not go back to bed! Let's go to the waterfall!" Mehmed almost fell off his chair in delight. Well, we prayed *fajr* in the yard and then everybody got dressed (Taqwa wanted a scarf that would match her red sweater). Then we piled into Baba's and Uncle Furqan's cars and we sped off down the road. It was so exciting to be out and about at that hour. It was still dark when we left, but as we drove along we soon started to see the shapes of the trees and bushes beside the road, and then rosy and lavender and even greenish streaks in the sky, and by the time we got to the road that leads into the waterfall, the sun was coming up. It was a brand new day. At the waterfall Taqwa's father put her up on his shoulders and carried her off into the woods. Her mother came and put her arm in mine and walked with me along the narrow grassy path, which was still wet with dew. "Thanks, Nur, you have been so kind to all of us. How can I ever thank you?"

She wanted to thank me, Buraq! I told her I hadn't done anything. It popped into my head while I was talking to her that Taqwa really is a lovely girl and I said I believe Allah loves her in a special way.

The waterfall loomed up in front of us, but Taqwa's mom stopped walking and pulled me close to her. She told me how afraid she has been for her girl in this past year, how it has broken her heart to see her turn her back on her mother, on her family, on all the things they had loved and done, on Allah. *Subhanallah*, I felt this rush of relief and gratitude that Mama never had to endure things like that because of me and, for the first time, I realized how safe Mama is, right now ... nothing can hurt her, ever!

Taqwa's mom said she'd seen her daughter in a dream last night—in our house—in a meadow of green grass and wildflowers, with butterflies flitting around her. Butterflies, Buraq, can you believe it! I got goose bumps all over me, and it wasn't from the early-morning cold, either. She said Taqwa greeted her in the dream with a brilliant smile.

I said, "Auntie, what an incredible dream."

"Nur," she said, "I am so weak, please make prayers for me. Please make a dua that I will know what to do."

I pulled her close and hugged her. "I will, Auntie."

Taqwa's dad came dashing by with her still on his shoulders, squealing with delight, followed by Baba with Mehmed on his shoulders. Taqwa's mother called out to them in Arabic; whatever she said made them laugh, and her husband stooped down for Taqwa to slide off. She came running over and nearly knocked her mother down in a huge bear hug and they went off together to explore the waterfall. Wow … was this the same girl?

Baba came over to me, still carrying Mehmed, and put his arm around my shoulder, steering me towards the crashing water.

"My Nuri, you are so like your mother! I'm so proud and grateful to be your dad."

Suddenly Mama's sweet smell came back into my nose and her voice rang in my ears, and I knew then that I would see her again somewhere else, and I thought of the Prophet Muhammad, may Allah bless him and give him peace, waiting for us at the Pool in Paradise, just as Allah has promised us.

Tomorrow Taqwa and her parents will return to the other side of the world, and what will happen to her? How strange … somehow, after seeing her play with her family here, it seems that whatever happens in the future, nothing will ever be able to erase the victory she has won here. She has said Yes!

I will miss her! I have spent so much time thinking about her in the past weeks. But she is leaving me with a great gift, and I will never forget that. She is leaving me with the gift of *taqwa*, the attribute that brings the Garden close, the attribute that gathers the good of this world and the next. She has taught me the meaning of patience. She has made me see that nothing, absolutely nothing, will work except for saying 'yes' to Allah. And if you do that, everything else falls into place: *Everything*.

Mama! You said, "Wait. You will see. Allah is cherishing you!"

I've seen it, Mama!

I wonder, dear Buraq ... is *this* what it feels like, having wings...

Glossary

Acma—a soft, yeasty Turkish bun

Adhan—the Islamic call to prayer

Alhamdulillah—"all praise is due to Allah" (Arabic)

Annem—"my mother" (Turkish)

Bendir—a hand drum used throughout North Africa and Turkey

Buraq—the name of the riding animal that took Muhammad on his sacred 'night journey' from Makkah to Jerusalem

Eid (al-Fitr)—the Islamic holiday after Ramadan

Fajr—the pre-dawn prayer

Habibti—"my love" (Arabic)

Hafiza-Qur'an—a girl/woman who has memorized the Qur'an

Iftar—the meal after a fast

Illahis—sacred songs

Inshallah—"if Allah wills" (Arabic)

Kaaba—the sacred building in Makkah, Saudi Arabia. Referred to as the 'House of Allah'

Maghrib—the prayer after sunset

Mashallah—a word of appreciation for what Allah has willed

Nur—"sacred light" (Arabic)

Ottomans—the people, mainly from modern day Turkey, who once ruled most of the Islamic world in Asia, Europe, and Africa. They were at the height of their power between the fifteenth and seventeenth centuries.

Quaker—a primarily Christian group who practice a religion of simplicity and gratitude

Ramadan—the Islamic month of fasting. It is the ninth month in the Islamic calendar.

Sahur—the pre-dawn meal eaten before fasting

Simit—a small ring-shaped Turkish bread with sesame seeds

Subhanallah—"Glory to Allah" (Arabic)

Tajweed—the proper pronunciation of the Qur'an

Taqwa—used to refer to the care a Muslim has for obeying the rulings of Allah in Islam i.e. keeping a protective shield against what is harmful

Taraweeh—the special evening prayer during Ramadan